Hi Doni,

Thanks for being here today - Enjoy reading my book -

Dennis W. Chowen

Boss Mouse

By
Dennis W. Chowen

authorHOUSE™

1663 Liberty Drive, Suite 200
Bloomington, Indiana 47403
(800) 839-8640
www.AuthorHouse.com

First published by AuthorHouse 12/06/05

ISBN: 1-4208-9078-6 (e)
ISBN: 1-4208-9076-X (sc)

Library of Congress Control Number: 2005909510

Printed in the United States of America
Bloomington, Indiana

This book is printed on acid-free paper.

Dedicated to
Mrs. Cari Frazier
And her 2nd grade class
2004-2005

I
BOSS MOUSE FINDS A NEW HOME

It was a sunny, morning that day when the family of mice came to find their new home in the meadow. The journey had been a difficult one, as the wind blew so hard it was easy for the family to lose their way.

The self-elected leader was called Boss Mouse. He was a wise old mouse that had escaped being captured by many cats during his long life. The guidance and council he gave to all the mice in the family was always accurate and kept them from danger during many difficult times. He always had the answers for everyone in all their moments of crisis.

The family was looking for a meadow that had luscious grass, small grain plants and fields of corn that could be used for gathering their food. Of course, a source of water was important also, but not as much as a haystack to serve as the cover and protection for their new home.

Boss Mouse often would gather all the mice in one location and demand that they all pay attention to him as he instructed them in what to do. He told them the stack of hay must be in an open field and not close to the other farm animals or the buildings.

"Cats and rats live in those buildings," he said, "and cats love to eat mice!"

Most of the time all the mice would respectively listen to Boss Mouse, but one little mischievous mouse thought he had other or more important things to worry about.

Boss Mouse had sent a couple of scout mice out in advance to search for the perfect location where the mouse family could raise their children, play freely without the fear of any cats, and have a continued supply of food. The two scout mice reported that evening to Boss Mouse that they had found a perfect location. A little stack of hay between fields of grain and puddles of water should serve their needs. The ground under the haystack was soft so they could make burrows in the ground for homes, and tall grasses were in good supply.

The scouts were pleased when Boss Mouse called all the mice together and reported the good news.

Boss Mouse, when making major decisions, would sit up very tall, groom his six long whiskers, brush his soft grey fur, clear his throat and announce the news. Everyone knew that when Boss Mouse cleared his throat it was time to listen.

Mrs. Mouse was especially interested in what Boss Mouse had to say, as she had a large family, all boys, which at times was very difficult to manage. Miffit was her next to the youngest and most demanding one of all. He was always, or so it seemed, getting into or just getting out of trouble. Miffit was a special little guy as he was born with only five and one-half whiskers. All the other mouse family members had six just like their grandpa, Boss Mouse. His friends and family often asked Miffit:

"What happened to you?"

2

"How come you have one short whisker?"

He never really could give an answer that satisfied anyone at all, so he just said, "It makes me special because you don't have only five and one-half whiskers." Other than one whisker being shorter than the other five, Miffit was a very normal mouse.

"He was much more adventurous, however, than all the other mice," Mrs. Mouse often said.

After the mice had found their way under the haystack, it was a very busy time getting all set up and ready for living. Older and braver mice had to search for food sources, while the younger boy and girl mice had to burrow in the soft ground making their nests and home. Boss Mouse was not surprised that squabbling and arguing was taking place. Some mice felt that the other groups had better or easier burrows to clean and prepare, while another might feel he had more work to do than his friends did.

It is not easy being born into a mouse family. The little ones are born with their eyes not yet opened and are very dependent upon mom and dad for their food and shelter. Then when one family member demands more attention than another does, it takes parenting skills and special development for mom and dad to rear their family. Even at birth, Mrs. Mouse knew that one of her children was unique because of the half whisker.

Boss Mouse asked some of the older boy mice to go into the meadow in search of food. Boss Mouse had instructed that any mice sent on errands or food search should be especially watchful for cats. He had given them all the training they should need to make sure if they saw any cat, how to escape and return home unharmed.

Each mouse had been through a sufficient amount of training, Boss Mouse felt, so he asked Miffit to go along to learn from the other older and wiser mice. Miffit sure was willing to go along, but the other mice were cautious and suspicious of what he might do or the trouble he could bring to the whole mouse family.

Since the family had worked very hard, they were all hungry for seeds of grain and grass to chew on that evening. Each worker had to bring in the seeds the best way he could, by either dragging them along the ground or filling the pouch in his mouth with seeds. It was always risky to hunt for food as birds flying overhead were constantly soaring in the air and could easily spot a mouse in an open field. Once spotted, birds will make a dive toward the ground and with their sharp claws pick up a mouse and be gone. That poor mouse will never be seen or heard from again. That did not bother Miffit one bit, as he opted to play some mouse games he learned from his friends, instead of hunting for food.

II
Trouble For Miffit

Miffit had gone unnoticed for several minutes when the mice heard a faint but distinct 'mew' nearby. From their training, they knew they must remain silent and motionless to avoid being seen by the cat. Boss Mouse had instructed all the mice since a very early age, what skills were necessary to escape most of the cat's tricks. However, this cat was the biggest, scariest, ugliest, and grey mixed with black, that anyone had seen.

The 'mew, mew' grew louder as the cat spotted Miffit playing all alone. It is the most dangerous time being alone when a cat is present, and they all understood that, but Miffit did not realize that the cat was between him and the burrows under the haystack!

That nasty old scary cat was mean and ugly. It had only one thing on its mind, and that was to catch a mouse for his meal. Just when the cat had Miffit in its paw, Miffit gouged the cat with its sharp teeth causing the cat to withdraw his paw and drop Miffit.

Boy, oh boy, did Miffit run! Nevertheless, that mean and ugly cat could run faster than Miffit! Just as Miffit found the burrow at the edge of the haystack, the cat slapped the ground with both paws trying to catch the escaping mouse. One of the cat's claws caught the end of Miffit's tail as he ran into the burrow. Miffit was in pain as his tail was broken, but for this time, he had escaped that ugly mean and scary cat!

After crying and feeling very sorry for himself, Miffit found the courage to return to the eating area where everyone was enjoying the seeds and berries gathered by the other workers. It was most difficult for him to approach Boss Mouse and explain why he had a broken tail. Boss Mouse was a wise and thoughtful leader. He said it was more important now to have your tail looked at by Mrs. Mouse than to discuss the details of why you were playing alone and not working like the other mice.

III
MRS. MOUSE FIXES MIFFIT

Mrs. Mouse had been counted on in the past to be the family doctor, make the disciplinary decisions, rear the children and arrange for the meals. From her training and practice in fixing many ailments for her children, she had Miffit better in just no time.

Miffit was so pleased that he was going to be able to play and have fun again. Mrs. Mouse was not able to keep Miffit's tail straight since it had been so badly broken by that ugly and mean cat. Miffit's tail now curved to the right making a half circle. It was no longer long and straight as in the past. Miffit knew that he was different with his one-half whisker, and now a hook in his tail made him really unique. He felt that he was very special now and would have to make the best of it, despite his little inconveniences.

A couple days later after Miffit had felt good enough to help with the morning chores; it was time for him to have some fun in the meadow. Prior to his being able to play the mouse games with the others in the group, he had to make sure that his nest was clean, and all his things were in the right places. It can be a lot of work to make sure all your play things are in the right place, he thought, so at times he would just pile them in a corner and sort through them later, when he needed them. It seems as though, however, later never came, as Miffit's room was always needing some improvement. Sometimes he would ask one of his brothers or sisters to give him a hand. He often would promise to help them back for their favors to him, but frequently was busy when they needed the help.

Mrs. Mouse had given all the mice their breakfast meal of seeds, nuts and berries that had been gathered the day before. She also made sure that that each one cared for his teeth and groomed his hair before he was allowed to go out for the fun games. Miffit asked if he could join the group, as this was the first time since breaking his tail. Mrs. Mouse requested that he see Boss Mouse before going with the other mice for their morning in the meadow. Going to see Boss Mouse could be upsetting and frustrating, Miffit felt, but this time he hoped it would be different. After all, he was just going out to play with the other members of the family. How could that hurt?

"Come in," said Boss Mouse, as he sat on his chair, grooming his silky, long, black, beautiful six whiskers. Boss Mouse always looked so neat, just as if he had been to the groomer, but Miffit knew that was not possible.

"Ok," said Miffit, "I am on the way in."

Boss Mouse was mysteriously quiet, as his shiny and beady black eyes seemed to look right through Miffit that morning. Miffit was really scared to talk to Boss Mouse. Nevertheless, Miffit knew that Boss Mouse was an understanding and thoughtful leader. He would not intentionally cause harm to any of the mice in the entire group. Miffit began to quiver and tremble with fright, even before Boss Mouse had any chance to say a thing to him.

"So, Miffit, would you like to tell me how you got your tail to be hook-shaped? I am interested in comparing what Mrs. Mouse has told me with what you have to say." Miffit began telling Boss Mouse what had taken place, and after a short while, Miffit was making apologies for not listening to instructions on avoiding those ugly cats. Boss Mouse encouraged Miffit to continue because Miffit was self-reflecting on how he had not minded and listened to his elders.

After what seemed like one-half of a day, but it really was only a few minutes, Boss Mouse offered Miffit a few suggestions to avoid having that happen again. Miffit, for one time in his life, did pay attention to the guidance given by Boss Mouse that day. He did not want to repeat that painful process of narrowly escaping the paw of that nasty old ugly cat, and almost losing a portion of his tail. Miffit was so pleased when he heard Boss Mouse tell him he could leave now. Boss Mouse continued to groom his beautiful coat of silky gray fur, and polish his long black whiskers. Miffit hoped that one day he could be wise like Boss Mouse.

Miffit was so happy that he jumped and skipped as he was leaving the burrow to join with the other mice to play the games with them. He was in such a hurry that he missed their secret passageway to the meadow and was crossing a grain field when his tail hooked on several strands of grain stocks. All the other mice had long straight tails that trailed directly behind each mouse leaving a line in the dirt. It was easy to follow the trail of any mouse, just follow the line that was between two feet and you could find any mouse in the pack. However, for Miffit, since he had broken his tail and it had a hook in the end, the story was entirely different.

While trying to join the other mice that morning, Miffit's tail got hooked on some grain stocks. He was not use to having a hook at the end of his tail. He liked his long straight one before that tragic event with the ugly cat. Miffit had to be so very careful everywhere he went because his tail was constantly getting hooked around weeds, grass, and everything else everywhere he went. When his tail hooked something behind him Miffit just went around and around in a circle. Every time he would lunge forward, he

would turn in another circle. The harder he tried, the faster around and around he went, but only in a circle. He tried so many, many times that a cloud of dust was around him from all his four paws clawing and scraping, trying to go some place but he just could not!

Miffit was trapped and had no way to get out. The more he called for help to his family of friends, the more worried he became. He knew that if his family could hear him, and so could that mean old ugly cat. Miffit wondered and worried about what he could do. He remembered from his training, that Boss Mouse said when in danger just remain quiet, close your eyes and be motionless. Boss Mouse had told him and all the others that a cat can detect motion and movement easily, but they have difficulty in identifying lifeless items, even if it is an animal or bird. It was most difficult for a mischievous mouse to remain perfectly still, especially when fearing for his own life.

Just as the sun was setting in the Western sky, and nearly dinner time in the burrow, Miffit heard what he thought was a familiar voice. The voice was so soft and faint, that for a moment Miffit thought he was hearing things. But it was not his imagination, instead, sure enough; it was his friends from home.

Boss Mouse, when checking all the activities of the day, noticed that Miffit had not returned from the field games that afternoon, so had sent out some others to find him. Fortunately, for Miffit they had arrived just as that ugly old mean cat's mew was heard in the near distance. All the mice stood still, motionless and quiet with their eyes shut and could hear the mew, mew, and mew. The sounds were getting softer and softer so they knew that that ugly old mean cat was traveling away from them.

"Good news for them!" they said.

Boss Mouse had given the mice a few suggestions on how to assist Miffit, should he be in some sort of trouble. Boss Mouse knew how mischievous Miffit could be and had thought in advance on solutions to what might be the problem. The other mice began to chuckle when they saw the shallow ditch in the form of a circle around the stock of grain. They knew Miffit had gone around and around so many times he had worn a path in the form of a narrow ditch all the way around the grain stock. The mice simply told Miffit that all he had to do was back up and turn the other direction and his tail would no longer be hooked to the grain. Miffit had become so excited and afraid that he was going to get caught by the ugly mean cat, he just did not think of the obvious.

Miffit was embarrassed and slightly red in the face, but since it was turning dark, the other mice did not notice. Of course, Miffit was not going to admit to the other mice that he could not figure out how to unhook his crooked tail. He was thinking real fast about another answer to tell Mrs. Mouse and Boss Mouse that evening during their dinnertime.

It is not fun eating dinner being worried about what you will have to answer following the meal. The seeds and nuts were very tasty today, Miffit was thinking. He wondered who had done all the work and gathered the food while he was going around in circles hooked to a stock of grain. For only a moment, he had a slight feeling of guilt, because he enjoyed playing and finding troublesome things to do rather than hunting for food. Miffit immediately quit his daydreaming when Boss Mouse asked him how his day had been. Miffit did not know just how much to tell or where to begin. Simply stated, Miffit just said "Oh fine". It was difficult for Boss Mouse not to laugh aloud, but he chuckled for a moment under his breath

After a good night of rest, it was again time to gather more food for the next few days. The night air was getting cooler now, leaves were dropping from the trees, and drinking water was more difficult to find. A family of mice cannot store water for drinking later. Water is the most important part of the family diet. Mice cannot get along without water for one day, but can manage on one meal of nuts and seeds every other day. Boss Mouse had trained all the mouse family on methods to find water even during the coldest times. He had taught them that they could just stick their tongue on blades of grass and sip the dew that had formed from cool night air. After water had become ice, a mouse learned that he could nibble and chew on the ice and when brought into his mouth and would melt, it too, was a way to quench his thirst.

IV
Boss Mouse Trains Mice To Bark

Early that morning Mrs. Mouse had asked the mice to gather some wheat, oats, and barley grains for the evening meal. It was always better that they worked in groups rather than as individuals. When a cat spots several mice, he would sometimes become confused about which mouse to try to catch. By the time, the ugly cat made a selection on which mouse to catch; all the mice had run every direction and left the cat with disappointment. It was a learning experience each time food was gathered. It seemed like between birds flying above, cats peering on every corner, and larger rodents always looking to catch a mouse, gathering a meal was a life-threatening event. That did not bother Miffit as he has his own plan. "Play now and eat later", he thought. "Let the others do the work". He always thought of himself first, family and friends next and food was his last choice. Miffit did not worry about anything, he was a carefree and careless mouse that chose not to prepare for tomorrow. "Just enjoy each day," he thought.

Boss Mouse had gathered all the mouse family together for a very important meeting the next afternoon. Whenever Boss Mouse asked all the mice to be present, they knew it was very important. Everyone had wondered during breakfast just what Boss Mouse would be telling all the family of mice. Miffit nearly had it figured out since his run in and bout with the mean old ugly cat caused him to have a broken tail, and he nearly was caught again the other day.

Everyone one had their special place to sit during those important meetings called by Boss Mouse. They were all expected to be in their selected positions and quiet when he entered the room where the meeting was held. Out of respect, most of the mice would stand up until Boss Mouse had taken his seat. All the mice held so much respect for Boss Mouse, as he had led the family out of many dangerous dealings with animals that prey on mice. Only the wisdom given from Boss Mouse to the family had given the happy life, as they knew it. When Boss Mouse addressed the group, they listened and learned from his experience as he told them how to deal with danger.

Boss Mouse said that the old ugly mean cat was spending a lot of time near the entrance on the West side of the haystack recently. It was going to be necessary to trick the cat into thinking there might be a dog barking in the area.

"If we all work together using my plan we can do just that; trick that cat into thinking we are dogs barking. I have a special plan that we can try", Boss Mouse said. "To try my plan we will need to have the bravest mice of all gather some special grains of wheat and barley and bring them here to me. "How many brave mice do we have here today?" said Boss Mouse.

Only a few of the older boy mice waved their paws showing support for the new plan. Boss Mouse said that they must go beyond a safe distance from the burrows in their haystacks to a place that only very bright green stocks of grain are growing. You can identify these green stocks because they are very near the underground spring of water that continues to make them lush and fruitful.

"One or two of the bravest mice will act as scouts," Boss Mouse said. "These two very brave mice will leave just before the sun comes up in the early morning and find this special green stock area. When you arrive, safely crawl up the stocks and gather seeds that are dark in color. Do not cut the stocks down and leave them on the ground. Birds flying above are watching to see how grain stocks are disturbed and might spot you. Make sure you only bring back to the main group dark colored seeds. Return as quickly as possible following each other very closely, keeping each other in your sight at all times. When you return I can tell you how the other mice will help."

Miffit wanted to be one of the scouts and even volunteered to do so, but this time he was not selected. Miffit had the reputation of not doing what he was told, and often times took nothing seriously at all. The other family of mice knew this, so that is the reason he was not selected to be a scout.

Boss Mouse said that after a couple days of gathering those dark colored seeds, he would show how they could be used to scare that old ugly mean cat. The two scouts brought a few seeds to Boss Mouse. Boss Mouse told them the seeds had to remain in a dark moist room for two and one half days. Boss Mouse then asked the scouts to guide the other brave mice to the lush green grains of wheat and barley so more colored seeds could be used. It took several days to get enough of the seeds to conduct the experiment that Boss Mouse had told the mouse family. Gathering those seeds was very risky, as pheasants and grouse would try to eat any seeds that had been dropped by the mice. Fox and raccoons are always looking for meals of juicy meat, and those seed-eating birds attracted those larger animals that not only preyed on mice but also on birds.

Well, after a few days of gathering seeds and bringing them back to the burrows, Boss Mouse inspected each seed. All the seeds had to be dark in color and fully developed. After being in the dark moist room for two and one half days, Boss Mouse told all those very brave mice to meet him in the meeting room next to the West entrance to the haystack. Boss Mouse said each mouse was to put a few seeds in his or her mouth and chew, chew, chew and chew the seeds without swallowing them. He said the moisture from their mouths combined with the damp air in the dark room would cause the mice to have a growling sound in their voice rather that the squeaky high-pitched sounds they normally make. Boss Mouse told them when he gave them the signal to make sounds they would be very pleased and surprised to learn the sound they would be making.

Boss Mouse sent out one brave scout to be on the lookout for the ugly old mean cat. The scout signaled to Boss Mouse that the ugly scruffy mean cat was a few feet from their entrance, hiding in some blades of grass. Boss Mouse asked all the brave volunteers to get very close to the entrance but not so birds or that ugly cat could see them.

"When I give the signal," Boss Mouse said, "all of you together, clear your throats at the same time.

When the signal was given, the sound made was a faint but distinct growling sound, much like a small dog. Boss Mouse asked all the mice to repeat and repeat that sound which resembled a growling dog. It was enough to distract the cat, for this time anyway, as it bristled up its mangled grey black fur and spurted a hissing sound. When cats make that type of sound, the mice knew it had been scared. The cat thought for a moment that a dog was going to chase it, so that ugly mean old cat ran away with fear.

The mouse family had been spared again from the threatening ugly cat, thanks to the strong leadership and experience of Boss Mouse. Miffit was sure relieved to learn that special trick that they all could use. As long as the cat did not see any mice and was in fear of a dog nearby, the plan worked. Boss Mouse had earned the respect of mice from that lesson he taught them. Boss Mouse now had more time to comb his thick grey fur, and brush his long six whiskers. Miffit wished he had long whiskers like Boss Mouse, but that was never going to be, since Miffit had one-half whisker. Many of the other mice would tease Miffit about his short whisker, and it bothered Miffit a lot, but there was not much he could do about it. He just told them he was born that way and would go off in another direction and play more of his games.

V

ROCKS AND LINES FORM WORDS

After an early breakfast and their training and instruction on survival and escape from the ugly old mean cat, the mice were allowed to play a couple games before gathering food for the rest of the day. Miffit was always the best at thinking of new games to play, as he never wanted to help with the chores of gathering food. When it was time to relax and play Miffit was the one that they all looked to for new ideas.

Miffit had suggested a game of 'hunt and crawl' between small rocks near the haystack. The farmers had cleared most of the rocks from their fields, but a few remained close to the haystack. It was real strange and interesting that morning to see how Miffit got his tail stuck under one of the little red rocks during their morning game. This time Miffit just dragged the rock under the haystack and asked for assistance in getting unhooked. Miffit never could figure out that all he had to do was just back up and he would be free. Mrs. Mouse was not pleased to see Miffit had dragged this rock in behind him. Mrs. Mouse began to remove the rock from his tail when she noticed a white line drawn diagonally across the rock. It was very mysterious looking she thought, as she was scolding Miffit for bringing in the rock.

Other family members were told to take the rock back to the place where it was when hooked to Miffit's tail. When the rock was placed back in the pile of rocks, the mice noticed interesting lines, dashes, and circles appeared to be on the surface of those rocks. To them it made no sense at all, just white scratches on red rocks. The more they thought about what they were seeing, the clearer their thinking became. It was time for them to bring in a couple of these rocks for Boss Mouse to examine. He would tell them what this meant and how to decipher these mysterious codes. The two mice hurried back to see Boss Mouse as quickly as they could.

The mice presented just two rocks to Boss Mouse for further examination. Boss Mouse made his decisions based on experience and knowledge. All the family of mice respected him for his wisdom and wise council. Like all the decisions before and those to follow, Boss Mouse conducted his ritual, this time he allowed some of the family of mice to observe.

The first and most important routine conducted was to brush his rich thick fur to ensure every hair was in place so he looked his very best. He brushed, brushed and brushed until he was completely groomed the way he liked. Next was the combing of his six long black whiskers. Each of his six whiskers had to be in their exact place. Two whiskers were curved upward, two downward, and the other two were sticking straight out from his face. After a special waxing and combing with a secret formula that kept all his whiskers in place, Boss Mouse could think about the problems.

"So, where were these rocks?" he asked.

The two mice replied, "They were just on the East side of the stack a few yards away. One was accidentally hooked to Miffit's tail during our early playtime today when we first noticed it. We brought in a couple for Mrs. Mouse to look at," they said.

Boss Mouse was sitting so very tall and straight in his chair; his eyes were in clear focus as he scrutinized those mystery lines on the rocks. This decision came rather quickly, they all felt. Boss Mouse said that these rocks when lined up precisely and exactly and viewed from higher in the air, would give us a message.

17

"We must immediately climb to the highest spot we can find to see if we can read the words. If the rocks are far enough from the haystack and we are high enough on the top of the haystack, we might be able to understand the message."

One of the mice suggested they climb a tree to be higher in the air. Boss Mouse looked very sternly and stared just for a moment at that mouse that had made that suggestion. Boss Mouse would never insult or ridicule anyone intentionally. He always had the right combination of words to say that let you know about your mistake.

Calmly and distinctly Boss Mouse responded by saying, "Yes, you could climb a tree, but that mean old ugly cat can climb must faster and efficiently than you can. In no time, you would be his next meal. None of us wants that to happen. We must carefully climb to the highest parts of the stack and see if we can read the letters on the rocks."

Signs of fall were everywhere. Leaves were falling from the trees. Farmers were finishing their fall work prior to winter arriving. Some were picking their corn, while others were cutting their last crop of grass and hay. Some of the mice could hear "Bang, Bang" in the distance and knew that hunters were shooting at wild pheasants and turkeys flying from field to field searching for food. Other mice observed flocks of geese above the clouds, floating in the air moving in their V formations to their Southern homes for the winter. It was a busy time for the farmers and an important time for the mouse family to gather their food.

Finally, after a long time, a couple of mice reached the top of the haystack. It had been a tough journey for the short-legged mice to crawl up through the snarls of dry grass and hay leaves. Each time they got a little higher, they would slip back a few more inches in the slick and dry stems and blades of grass. Miffit was no help at all to anyone. He made little tunnels and trails in and around the haystack for some new games for his friends. He thought it more fun to explore new routes between burrows using passages in between leaves and grasses. The other mice were not amused when Miffit complicated their journey to the top of the haystack with all his extra new trails to discover.

The mice reported that they just were not high enough in the air to decipher what the meaning of the lines on the rock meant. No matter how they studied the white lines or from what position on the top of the haystack they looked, the lines just made no sense at all. They could clearly see the rocks and the lines on the rocks but could not understand any message that was being given to them.

It was time again for Boss Mouse to offer more information to the mouse family. Everyone was eager to understand and learn about those mystery lines and what they possibly could mean. Miffit suggested to the group, "Perhaps it was just some chicken or turkey that was scratching for food that made the lines on the rocks." Someone else thought it could have been that the mean old ugly cat sharpening its claws. Most of the group hoped it had not been the ugly old scruffy cat sharpening its claws, because that meant the cat would be hunting for more food. "Let us refer this to our leader, Boss Mouse," they all agreed.

During the meeting of the family of mice, Boss Mouse shortened his ritual, somewhat. He had not paid that much attention to his thick coat of gray fur like in the past meetings. Miffit had noticed that a few hairs on the back of Boss Mouse were not in place, but it looked like some food was stuck to them. Miffit did not focus on what Boss Mouse was telling the group, as he was thinking about those hairs with food stuck to them. Each of the six whiskers was in perfect condition. Two up, two down, and the other two straight as an arrow. Miffit wished he could use some of that secret formula on his five and one half whiskers. Perhaps enough of that secret formula would lengthen that short whisker of his. "Sure would help him," he thought, because so many mice teased him about his short whisker.

Boss Mouse gently cleared his throat and began to speak softly and slowly. It was so quiet in the meeting room when Boss Mouse was speaking, a mouse could hear a feather drop. Miffit had an itch on the end of his nose and either had to sneeze or scratch it. Neither choice was a good one because when Boss Mouse spoke it was impolite to make a sound or move no matter how important it seemed to be. Without any warning Miffit did sneeze, and rather loudly. Without hesitation, Miffit apologized for the interruption. Boss Mouse paused for a brief moment, and began telling the mouse family what they had to do to understand the lines on the red rocks.

VI
DUCKS HELP THE MOUSE FAMILY

"We must call on a few brave mice to take a journey in the air using a couple ducks for the flight. When the ducks are in the air to the right height, these brave mice can look down from that distance and read the letters on the red rocks. It is important that the mice selected be able to remain silent during the flight. During this flight, the ducks will hold a corn stock between their bills. The brave mice will clamp their teeth to the corn stock and hang on. If either of the mice says one word or opens his mouth he will fall off the corn stock and never be seen again." Boss Mouse said, "We must now activate my plan to locate a duck and ask for the ride."

How do you locate and catch a duck, Miffit wondered? During all his playtime, he had seen cats, turkeys, geese, chickens and a few other wild birds, but no ducks. He knew better than to ask Boss Mouse on the tricks of catching ducks, so at least temporarily agreed to help find a couple of ducks. Boss Mouse had told the group that the favorite food for a duck was corn. Therefore, Boss Mouse asked several mice to find the corn stocks, nibble off a few kernels, and bring them back to the meeting room. Since the farmers were now harvesting the corn and storing it in their bins, ears and kernels were becoming scarcer. In addition, what few cobs of corn that fell off the farmers' wagons were being eaten by wild turkeys, pheasants and other wild game birds. It was not only dangerous work because that ugly old mean cat was always looking for a mouse to eat, but that the colored corn like Boss Mouse wanted gathered was first choice of food by everyone else.

Some of the mice were successful in finding the kernels that were red, orange and brown in color. It was so tempting to chew and nibble on the kernels that were to be brought back to the meeting room. Miffit could not resist chewing his collection of kernels, so when he arrived at the meeting room it was just pure luck if he had but one kernel left! He did not help that much, but Boss Mouse said, "Every little bit does help and we need all the kernels we can get". After a couple days of very demanding work gathering the corn to attract the ducks, Boss Mouse explained how to make his plan work. He said, "Tomorrow morning, immediately following our breakfast meal, everyone will come to the meeting room. At that time, I will tell you my plan".

Many of the mice were very anxious to meet after breakfast to hear just what Boss Mouse had to say. He was such a wise and knowledgeable leader. Everyone was so proud of him and the decisions he made for the family of mice. Mrs. Mouse always had to chuckle just a little to watch Boss Mouse brush and comb his thick gray fur. She often wondered why the decisions could not be made without all that fuss, but understood why the ritual was conducted.

Boss Mouse said, "First of all, several mice will have to gnaw off the grass to make a clearing in the field. After a clearing is made, then the worker mice will go out and appropriately lay each kernel of corn in neat rows to form words. The words will be recognized from a high distance in the air. It is not possible to read the words from the ground as you are placing the red, orange and brown kernels to form the words."

"Since the favorite food for ducks is corn," Boss Mouse said, "We must lay all the kernels in lines to spell the word CORN. When flying in search of food the ducks will notice the letters saying corn and immediately land on the ground to investigate. After we have done this for a couple of times, we then will be able to ask the duck for help in exchange for more of their favorite food, which is corn."

After Boss Mouse determined that enough corn kernels had been gathered to form the word, he asked each worker mouse to begin chewing down the grass for a clearing. After the clearing had been made, other mice in the family would begin to form the letters using kernels of corn to attract the flying ducks. Boss Mouse had asked everyone to cooperate and get this done quickly. The entire clan of mice was very anxious to get help from the ducks so they could join them in the air and learn what the white lines in the red rocks had to say.

A couple days later, while observing from high on the haystack, a couple of scouts noticed that a couple of ducks were circling above the word CORN that they had made. This was an exciting time for the mouse family. Immediately, the scouts ran in to tell Mrs. Mouse what they had seen. Mrs. Mouse climbed up in the stack to see what she could see. All she saw were two turkeys walking over to the cleared grass area in search of seeds to eat. It was a huge disappointment for all the mice when in just a few short minutes the turkeys had eaten most of the kernels of corn. Of course, the ducks noticed it before anyone else did and flew off in another direction to find their meal for the day. The mice agreed that they would try the plan Boss Mouse had given them, before reporting to him what they had observed that afternoon.

After one more try of getting a duck to recognize that food had been gathered and placed for them in neat little rows, the plan seemed to work. Several mice had been watching all day very quietly and patiently for some ducks to land on the ground next to the corn and begin eating the kernels. Food this time of the year was not easy to find. The corn had all been picked and placed in secured storage bins. What had been dropped during harvest had been eaten by game birds that lived in the area. In addition, it was so easy for them to walk in and around the fields on the farm and eat all the corn. None seemed to be left for birds that migrate and fly high above the ground.

When birds are flying above and see food on the ground spelling their favorite food, they stop by to investigate.

Early that evening just before sundown two young ducks began to circle above the corn the mice had prepared for them. The other game birds had given up their search for food for the day and were roosting early that night. That was fortunate for the two ducks that continued to circle lower and lower and finally land on the ground. They enjoyed their meal of tasty corn, and proceeded to fill their craw full of the sweet fresh picked corn kernels. What a treat it was to have found this clutch of corn, the ducks felt. All the way back to their home that evening they were making plans on how to lead the others back again tomorrow for more delicious corn.

The two scouts that observed the ducks eating the corn on the ground were excited. They eagerly reported what they had seen to Mrs. Mouse. She told them they should wait for one more day to make sure more ducks came back for more of that tasty corn. It was difficult for these two scouts to get any sleep that night. They wondered and wondered if tomorrow the same two ducks would return for more food. They also thought about how they might talk these ducks into taking a couple mice on a ride with a corn stock stuck in their mouths. After asking each other several questions about what to do and how to do it tomorrow, they drifted off to sleep.

After breakfast of tasty nuts, grains and seeds, the scouts went immediately to the top of the haystack to watch for ducks. All the worker mice were very busy gathering and placing more of the bright colored red, orange and brown seed in neat rows to spell CORN again. Their hope was that the turkeys would not come by today for an early morning snack like they did yesterday.

Within a few minutes after the seeds were in place a large flock of ducks was circling above the place where the kernels had been placed.

"Be very quiet and do not move so we do not disturb these ducks," one scout said.

They were so very quiet, sat motionless and waited to see where the ducks would land. Within moments, a group of five or six ducks landed and began eating the corn. "Now, how can we talk with them and coax them for a ride they asked each other. This is something we need to discuss with Boss Mouse, and soon. We are running out of choice kernels of corn to lure the ducks in to coming to our haystack. Kernels are very hard to find since all the farmers have harvested their crops this season. Fall is here and winter is coming. What can we do?

VII
MIFFIT'S HOOKED TAIL BECOMES USEFUL

Mrs. Mouse approached Boss Mouse with the current status of what the scouts had reported to her.

Boss Mouse said, "Call a meeting of the entire mouse family before our noon lunch and play time. At that time, I can prepare and present my plan to the group. I think you will be pleased with the results," Boss Mouse said.

Mrs. Mouse wanted to request deletion of the ritual Boss Mouse routinely conducted prior to any meeting, since this was a very important one. She was in no position to ask such a favor or request from Boss Mouse. Mrs. Mouse just shrugged her head and shoulders and prepared herself for what would happen next.

Following a rather suspicious look from Boss Mouse over the mouse family, he surprised them all by asking Miffit to come to his side. Miffit was shaking in his skin with fright. To be in the immediate presence of Boss Mouse was something special, but when Boss Mouse asked Miffit by name to come forward, WOW.

Miffit reported to Boss Mouse as requested, clearly wondering what he would be doing. Boss Mouse asked Miffit to get the brush and begin brushing his thick gray fur.

"While you are brushing my fur and getting me to look special and important, I can be using my special formula on my whiskers at the same time. We can save time," Boss Mouse said.

Always Boss Mouse prepared two for pointing up, two other whiskers pointing down and the other two straight out. This time four whiskers were pointing up and two were straight out. The group noticed the difference immediately. All the mouse family was perplexed. The entire group waited for the wisdom that always came from Boss Mouse. He was a very special leader who had kept all the mice from danger through many generations. Everyone counted on him again for assistance in how to coax the ducks for a ride in the sky.

"We have two choices," Boss Mouse said. "Both are good options. To begin, we can ask two ducks to fly above holding a corn stalk with a couple mice clinging to the stalk, flying through the air. That option requires the mice not to open their mouth during the flight, because if they do they will lose their grip on the stalk and fall to the ground and never be seen again. Another option would be for the duck to fly above the ground and then read the word or words and tell us what they say or mean." Boss Mouse said either option would work, so his decision this time would be based on what most of the mouse family had to think.

Most of the mice thought it would be better if a couple mice took a ride on the corn stalk with the ducks. They felt they could find two mice that would not talk during the ride. Boss Mouse asked for volunteers to take the trip. The first one that volunteered was, yes, no other than Miffit. Miffit said he could use the hook in his tail as a way to hang on to the corn stalk. That way he would be looking down and could read the words. In addition, he would not have to be quiet. A couple other mice volunteered also. The final decision would come from Boss Mouse. His decisions were always final, not contestable, and filled with knowledge and wisdom. Boss Mouse said he liked the idea of using the hooked tail as a grip rather than using their teeth. The idea of being able to look down and see the words was a good idea.

The two ducks agreed to take Miffit into the air only if they were promised to have enough kernels to eat for their family over the next couple of days. Boss Mouse took inventory of the amount of kernels remaining in their burrow and determined there was a sufficient amount of corn remaining. It would require each worker mouse to work extra hard over the next couple of days to gather additional seeds and grain to feed the hungry mouse family. A mouse can eat nearly its body weight in seeds and grain every day. That would require an extra effort by all the mice, but well worth it. It was agreed that early the next morning the ducks would take Miffit on the ride in the air.

It sure was a good thing that the wind was not blowing and there were no clouds to block the view from below to see the lines on the rocks. Miffit knew that the entire mouse family depended on him to read the lines in the red rocks. He sure hoped that he would be able to understand what it all meant. He thought back to his early schooling and wished he had paid more attention to his teachers and did all the homework they had requested.

"I am ready now for the ride in the air, so let us go!" Miffit said to his newfound duck friends!

Miffit made sure that his tail was firmly placed over the corn stalk that morning before the ride with the two ducks.

"This time," Miffit exclaimed, "there is an advantage to having a hook in my tail!" "Not too many other uses for a mouse with a crooked tail," he thought, "so I had better take advantage of this one."

It was a bright sunny day with little to no wind that morning, and Miffit was glad of that. He was able to look down from above and read the lines drawn on the red rocks to find the answer to the puzzle everyone had wondered about. He was glad to be in the position to help the family of mice this time. Miffit was usually the one causing trouble and not helping the mouse family.

The lines began to form words on the rocks. Miffit was amazed to learn that when so far away the lines did make sense. He signaled to the ducks that he was ready to return now since he had learned what the lines meant. He was a bit confused however, since the two letters he could recognize did not make any sense to him. He knew that he would report his sightings to Boss Mouse, who always had an answer. After the ducks flew back to the ground and Miffit thanked them for the ride, he immediately ran into see Boss Mouse. It was an exciting time, as all the family of mice awaited the news.

Miffit said he recognized two letters, a big '0' and then another letter much like a little 'g'.

"When you combine these two letters," Miffit said, "They make the sound like 'og' in the word fog."

He was not familiar with that word and asked Boss Mouse what he thought it might be. Boss Mouse was so amused, he chuckled loudly.

"How could you not know what the two letters mean?" Boss Mouse said. "Reverse the order of the words and you have a clear signal to the family of mice – GO". Miffit was disappointed to think that he did not figure that out by himself.

Boss Mouse said, "We must take action on moving from our comfortable home under this stack to some other place. Alert all the mouse family early in the morning!"

VIII
MOUSE FAMILY MOVES AGAIN

Even before breakfast that morning, the word had spread all over the burrows about the words on the rocks. Rumors were spreading from tunnel to burrow and mouse to mouse like haze across the meadow. So many questions with few answers, it seemed. All the family of mice was on the highest alert. Although mandatory attendance was required for the morning meeting, it was not necessary because everyone wanted to be there to learn about the plan for relocation from the safe home they all knew, to the uncertainty of where to go and how to get there.

During the gathering for the meeting, a couple mice said they heard big, big machines near their haystack home. This meant only one thing - the farmers were going to scoop up the big heavy stack on their trucks and trailers and haul them to their farmyard. Each year in the fall time, it is common for all the farmers and ranchers to move their stacks near the corrals and buildings to feed their livestock during the winter. Boss Mouse knew this was going to happen but hoped that it would be later this year since the weather had been so nice. He was not ready to move the entire mouse family with such short notice. "And just where will they go to this time," he wondered?

This was the first time that Boss Mouse did not conduct the ritual prior to making any announcements to the entire group. He had a frazzled look on his face, worry in his eyes, and he did not sit in a straight position like in the past. His six whiskers were in order, however; two pointed down, two pointed up and the other two straight out. He managed to use his secret formula again without anyone taking notice. "Too much anticipation and excitement to worry about whether his whiskers were straight or crooked," they all thought.

Mrs. Mouse had the most to worry about. Moving a large family across an open meadow any time of the day was an opportunity for a fox or cat to catch a mouse with little effort. She had worried most of the night about how she was going to save her large family while moving from one place to another. She knew that Boss Mouse was a good leader and had to trust his judgment. "It was all in his hands she thought," as she began to gather up all her belongings to make this important move.

It seemed to be earlier than usual when the farmers approached the haystack that morning and all the confusion began. The scouts, Mrs. Mouse and Boss Mouse had early warning when they heard the loud roar of a truck and trailer closer and closer to the haystack. They all knew it could be a disastrous day if they did not follow instructions and make a hasty move from their burrows. Everyone was busier than ever trying to gather all they had and take with them. Miffit was not any help at all. He was more interested in seeing his friends and playmates than preparing to move from one place to the other.

The farmer backed up the huge trailer under the haystack and began to load it for the move back to his corrals. Smoke poured out from the pipes of the large truck and tractor as the haystack began to be loaded.

Boss Mouse signaled to everyone and said, "Now is the time to run as fast as you can!" "Follow me!" he said. "If you get lost or lose your way you can see where we have gone by following our trail. Remember that we have our tails straight out behind us leaving a clear path in the dirt to follow. That is why Miffit must be in the front of the line between Mrs. Mouse and me. The smoke from the tractor and truck along with the thick fog this morning will give us some protection from that mean old ugly cat."

Boss Mouse scurried from his comfortable huge burrow along with many other mice to find their new home.

"Just follow the mouse in front of you," he said. "Take hold of their tail if necessary, and do not lose sight of them. We must move quickly and swiftly traveling in the bottoms of ditches or cracks in the ground to avoid being seen by that ugly old cat. If anyone hears the mew or sees the cat, we will all form a circle and using our loudest voices, make sounds to scare it away. Let us hope the cat was well fed yesterday and not searching today for a quick meal."

Miffit was worried about where they would be eating the noon meal today and not helping at all. Boss Mouse firmly told him to get in the line and quit worrying about food today.

Rain clouds were forming above. The thick haze combined with the tractor and truck exhausts protected the mice from the cat's view for a few minutes. The farmers loaded the haystack on the trailer and began to drive off, when that old mean ugly and scruffy cat noticed a huge mole trying to escape. How fortunate that the cat's attention was directed to that fat old mole and not the line of mice moving toward the open meadow. The mole was large enough for a couple meals for the cat, and that ugly scruffy cat knew that, so began to pursue the mole for breakfast.

Moles are clever, quick, and vicious fighters. When that ugly old mean cat began to chase the mole, it had a fight on it hands. This daddy mole was the size of an average sized gopher. When the mole puffed up, and the hair on its back was standing on edge and showing all four front teeth, the ugly old mean cat had to think about how to trap this varmint. The mole stood on it back legs and clawed toward the approaching cat. This motion, for a moment stopped the cat in its tracks. Moles communicate using deep groan- like sounds when in distress or trouble. These sounds, when repeated rapidly, are much like sounds that a ventriloquist might do; that is, make you think the sounds are in a different place. This would cause confusion for the cat, as it would not know which way to look to find the mole.

Also, moles use their back legs to scratch the ground and throw sand or dirt into the eyes of the enemy when they are in danger. It is their method of escape, and this mole sure did throw a lot of dust in the eyes of the cat. By the time the cat had cleared the pebbles and grains of sand from its eyes, the mole had disappeared into one of the burrows used by the mouse family. It was a real tight fit getting into these small shallow tunnels, the mole thought, but a better choice than being squeezed in a clutching ugly cat's paw. The cat had given up its search for hunting for a mouse or mole today and would try to catch a bird instead. "That was just fine by the mouse and mole family," they all thought.

The breeze was beginning to blow a little harder now. The sun was peeping through the rain clouds and the haze and smoke was drifting off the meadow. This was not a good thing for the family of mice. They would have to move more rapidly than they had been during the early morning. It was a difficult time for the family of mice. Boss Mouse could not talk to all the mice behind him because he was concerned about what direction to lead his large family. He knew that if he went toward the area where the grass was short or the open meadow, they could be seen from birds of prey flying above. In addition, Boss Mouse knew that not only was there that mean old ugly cat in the area, but also wild fox often had been seen hunting for food. The best approach was to use tall heavy grass and very shallow ditches for the best protection.

IX
MIFFIT TAKES GOPHIE'S FOOD

It was just half past noon time when Miffit began to grumble about wanting something to eat. The apparent danger meant nothing to him at all. It was enjoyment and nourishment he wanted. He eagerly asked Mrs. Mouse when they could stop for water and some food. He knew that asking Boss Mouse for anything under these hectic conditions was not appropriate, so he continued to nag and nag Mrs. Mouse. She could not stress enough to Miffit, the importance of moving the entire family of mice to another location. Mrs. Mouse could not understand how Miffit could think of such things. She voiced her disgust and disappointment to Miffit, but he would not listen. He was only interested in himself and nothing else.

Within a very few minutes Boss Mouse had found dug out burrows and tunnels used by gophers and some prairie dogs. He asked the family of mice to stop for a rest and to find some seeds to eat before they traveled much further. Boss Mouse thought for a few minutes and decided to use these tunnels for their lodging for that night. He asked all those not standing guard for that mean old ugly cat, to see what they could find for food to eat.

Gophers and prairie dogs eat much the same thing that mice eat with a little more variety. Gophers are fast runners and travel long distances from their homes to find food for their families. Often they will dine on apples found on the ground or vegetables found around farmers' gardens. Prairie dogs do not move far from their homes above the ground. They use extensive underground thorough ways and connecting tunnels to gnaw the roots of grass, weeds and other plants for their main diet. Boss Mouse was aware that these newfound varmints always stored plenty of food for their family. Perhaps, he thought, if he explained the circumstances, he could talk them out of some food for the night. "What might I offer them in exchange for food?" he wondered.

The family of mice had to move to a safe place immediately. They knew that sitting on the ground they would soon perish from the birds of prey and the traveling fox. Without any permission, Boss Mouse moved his large family into the first gopher hole he had seen. He would ask permission later, he thought. It was fortunate that the striped gopher was a long way from his home in search of food that afternoon when the mouse family moved in for the evening. In just a short distance from the entrance hole the family of mice had noticed the storage bin used by the gopher. It was an awesome sight. Dried apples and other fruits, seeds piled high and so yummy looking, and then they saw the underground spring dripping water below. Boss Mouse had trained his family not to take something that did not belong to them. It was so temping as the mouse family was thirsty and hungry.

Miffit could not resist the temptation. He lunged forward into the dried fruit and began to have a taste of these prime stored tastes Boss Mouse was not quick enough to stop him in taking a bite or two. Boss Mouse was very displeased with Miffit and his actions that afternoon. He said that he would have special punishment for the misconduct of Miffit. The rest of the very hungry and thirsty mice listened to their leader and avoided eating the food gathered by someone else. Miffit said since the gopher was gone it would not notice just a few thing missing. Besides, we could replace what had been eaten with other grains and seeds we could gather. Boss Mouse again told him it was not right to take something that does not belong to you.

"You will be treated with favor if you ask permission," Boss Mouse said, "but thought of as a thief if not."

To the surprise of all the family of mice, the gopher arrived at the entrance to his home. The brown and green stripped gopher had never seen that many mice at one time or in one location. He stood at the entrance of his home with the food he had brought to put into the storage bin and instantly began asking questions. The gopher did not threaten or challenge any of the mice, he just wondered why so many of them and for what? The message was relayed to Boss Mouse who came to explain to the gopher what was taking place. It was a scary time for the family of mice. They knew their only hope was to have Boss Mouse negotiate a plan remaining the night for safety and food.

After a very brief introduction between Boss Mouse and the gopher, the discussion began to take place. Boss Mouse was wise and filled with experience and solutions to nearly every predicament. He was a creative thinker, excellent speaker and had an easygoing temperament. If an agreement could ever be reached at all, Boss Mouse could make it happen. His keen sense and ability to recognize and direct focus toward both sides coming to agreement, was one of his special talents. Boss Mouse wanted to look his best for this meeting, but had to rely on a quick fix for the six whiskers instead of using the special formula. They were not quite as sheen and reflective as he liked when using the formula, but it would have to do for today.

X
GOPHIE AND BOSS MOUSE MEET

The gopher was one of the younger juvenile gophers that just gone out on his own. He had been trained well by his parents in how to gather and store food. He also was raised by parents that cared about what he did and how to treat others. His parents told him that you help those in need if you can.

"What goes around," they told him, "comes around."

Boss Mouse had to explain to the family of mice that that means what you do to others would some day happen back to you. Therefore, if you are nice and kind to others, then others will repay you with kindness and goodness in return. How fortunate for the family of mice to have found that gopher hole that afternoon from so many to choose from. Boss Mouse had a very positive feeling about how the meeting would take place. He was somewhat perplexed, though, about how to explain or repay for the few bites Miffit had stolen from the storage bin.

The young gopher said his real name was Swifter, but his friends had given him a nickname of Gophie when he was a little fellow growing up. He went on to say that, the name had stuck with him during the last few months. He had been given that nickname because he goofed and fumbled around so much growing up.

Boss Mouse introduced himself as the leader of the mouse family. He told Gophie they had to move from their home under the haystack because the farmers were hauling the stacks to the corrals for the winter. It was necessary to find a new place to live, perhaps somewhat safer than where they had been. Boss Mouse said the entire family was always on the lookout for an old ugly mean cat that constantly chased their family. They had lived in fright the entire time they lived under the haystack. In fact, Miffit had his tail broken from that ugly old mean cat. That was the reason his tail now had a hook at the end.

After a period, Gophie told Boss Mouse they could spend the night in that area. He said gophers make networks of underground tunnels that join other family and friends so there would be plenty of accommodations for the entire family for a few days if they needed it. Boss Mouse was pleased to accept the gracious offer by his newfound friend, Gophie, and relayed the good news to the mouse family. Boss Mouse did inform Gophie of the fact that Miffit had eaten some choice seeds from the storage bin, but would restock the bin with newly gathered seeds. Gophie said it was not necessary, but Boss Mouse insisted that Miffit would bring back many more seeds for the storage bin than had been taken from it. Boss Mouse said it was important for the mouse family to learn not to take something that does not belong to them. Miffit was given the task to replenish the seeds. He was to begin gathering the seeds before and during the evening meal. Miffit missed his dinner as punishment for taking something not belonging to him.

XI
SECRET MAP TO A NEW WORLD

Gophie told Boss Mouse that this area was not safe to live in and they should seek a new home within a couple days. He said that so many prairie dogs and gophers live here that they were a food supply for the numerous fox and coyotes that constantly hunted them. He said the prairie dogs do not travel far from their underground tunnels in search of food like the gopher family. He said this caused the larger varmints to dig underground looking for food and catch prairie dogs. Gophie said that the mice would be safe for only a couple days because they are so much smaller than gophers or prairie dogs. Soon, fox, coyotes or birds flying above would be hunting them. Boss Mouse asked Gophie if he could direct the mouse family to a safe place to live.

Gophie said he heard about a new land not far from where they were now. It would not be easy to find he said because of the small stream and open fields that separate the two places. Gophie was told by his granddaddy that safe routes to the new place must be followed in order to not get lost and eaten by all the animals and birds that will prey on your family. Boss Mouse was most interested in how to get to the new land and where to find the maps.

Gophie told Boss Mouse "The secret map is on the underside of the belly of a turtle. All turtles have designs and patterns on their stomach," Gophie said, "this is how they can be told apart. You will know and recognize the turtle with the correct map on its stomach showing directions to the new land, when you reach the small stream. All turtles resemble one another in similar ways, but yet each is different with distinct markings or shapes they have had since they were hatched."

"Thus, this is how you may recognize the turtle with the map and directions to the new land. One turtle when hatching from the egg caught its right eye on a sharp portion of the shell. The shell caused its right eye to droop and blink constantly. To help this young turtle from being teased because its right eye blinked and drooped, the daddy turtle used the markings on its stomach as a map to a new and better place. The new place could only be found using the map on the stomach of the drooping eye turtle." The daddy turtle told so few about the map and the new land that hardly anyone knew about it. Only through folklore, customs and bedtime stories had Gophie learned about the new land and how to get there.

Boss Mouse was honored to think he had been told about the secret map to the new land. He pondered to himself, 'what goes around comes around', and began to find a place to rest for the evening.

"Oh!" Gophie said, "Don't be fooled by imposters"

It has been told that there is a huge snapping turtle in that region that catches all its food by blinking its drooping eye. When a stranger approaches the imposter with the drooping eye and asks about the map on its stomach, the snapper eats them!

Gophie said that his late and great uncle went in search of the map, but has never returned. "That was a couple seasons ago", he said.

Boss Mouse had a restful night after the food and advice provided to him by Gophie. "It will be difficult to lead the family of mice," Boss Mouse thought to himself. For starters, I do not know which way to go or how to get there. He must not reveal his feelings of uncertainty to the family of mice. If this would take place, the trust and confidence they had for him would be eroded. In the past, Boss Mouse had made decisions on experience, knowledge and his quick thinking ability. "I will do the same this time," he thought.

"I will use sound judgment and my creative thinking to take the family to the small stream where we can find the map," he said under his breath to himself.

Everyone had gathered for this meeting, with the exception of one mouse. Boss Mouse asked where Miffit was. Mrs. Mouse said that Miffit had worked most of the night gathering food to repay Gophie, and was still sleeping. Boss Mouse did forgive Miffit and his tardiness. He had remembered that Miffit had not only missed the evening meal to repay for his stealing the food, but worked the entire night as well. After a minimum amount of grooming and no special formula used on his six whiskers Boss Mouse laid out his plan to find the map on the stomach of the turtle.

"We will begin like we did on the move from the hay stack to Gophie's home," he stated.

"I will lead," Boss Mouse said. "Miffit will follow me. Mrs. Mouse follows Miffit, and all the others behind Mrs. Mouse. Keep each other in your sights at all times, and remember the name of the mouse in front and behind you. This will keep you from getting lost. We again will travel in very tall grass using shallow ditches as available to provide us protection from birds flying above and the many fox and coyotes hunting in the area. Since Gophie did not introduce us to any prairie dogs, we will not travel near those locations."

All during the first morning of traveling Boss Mouse wondered just how they would find the right turtle with the drooping eye. He did not have much experience with turtles but remembered that they spend most of their time in and under water. He did remember that he had seen them sitting on small logs in streams and ponds soaking up the sun. Boss Mouse also knew that turtles travel on land for food and often bask on banks near streams and ponds. Boss Mouse was a wise and thoughtful leader and felt more comfortable about his decision the farther the journey went.

Everything had gone so well for the traveling mice that morning. Even though the wind was blowing, enough clouds blocked the view of birds flying above so they could not see the migrant family moving slowly across the field below. The fox and coyotes in the area had found sufficient numbers of prairie dogs to hunt so they did not search for any mice that day. Oh how fortunate for the mouse family, Boss Mouse thought. "What a wonderful journey we are having," he told himself.

Miffit was the first to notice a rather large brown furry long tailed animal not far from them. Miffit used his high-pitched voice to signal to Boss Mouse that he had seen something. Boss Mouse gave his special silent signal alerting all the mice to remain motionless and silent.

"Do not breathe, move, or make a single sound," Boss Mouse said. "You will not be noticed or recognized if you do not move."

The entire line of mice followed the advice given of their wise and considerate leader. What seemed like several minutes passed before a huge hungry skinny long tailed rat crawled into a nearby hole in search of food. He failed to notice the mouse family! Boss Mouse gave the all clear sign and they began to travel on. He told the mouse family they must move rapidly and very quickly now to get out of sight of that rat.

Boss Mouse told the family of mice that rats do not have good reputations. They are cunning and crafty and will do anything they can to anyone to help themselves. "It would be better for us if we can avoid these ugly critters. We do not need any extra harm placed on us from the likes of a rat."

"The sun will be setting soon," Boss Mouse said. "We will need to find a safe place for the night. Within one more day of travel we will be able to see the stream and find the turtle. Everyone be on the lookout for our resting place tonight, as we will have to stop within a couple of hours. We can find some food when we arrive at our resting place for the night," he said.

Miffit never paid attention to the directions from Boss Mouse. He was always thinking of something else, mainly food and things to play with. He soon spotted some lush grass and tall weeds a short distance from the trail the mice were making. Miffit was thinking of some games to play using long stems of grass and short roots when he noticed what appeared to be unfamiliar colored dirt in front of them. Most of the soil he had seen was rich black earth that grew crops for the farmers. It was easy soil to dig in and more fun to play in he thought. The closer they came to this off colored soil he knew that it was leaves on the ground that had fallen from the huge oak trees. The variety of colors of leaves gave the appearance of the ground being orange, dark green, some dull reds and most browns. Miffit had hoped the family of mice could stay there tonight so he could play under and around all those leaves.

Boss Mouse noticed that Miffit was not keeping in line and must have been thinking about something else. When Boss Mouse noticed all the leaves that had fallen to the ground, it dawned on him that that must be what Miffit had been dreaming about. He knew that Miffit was thinking of playing in the leaves, but Boss Mouse was thinking of shelter for the night. Perhaps we can find some shallow tunnels at or near where the roots of the trees come out of the ground. Boss Mouse knew that trees live near a water supply. This would be a dandy place to spend the night, he thought. Since it was the fall season now the family of mice could use the leaves for covers over the openings for the tunnels they would sleep in. Additionally, if they had sufficient time the family could play games hiding and seeking in the piles of leaves. Boss Mouse wondered if he should compliment Miffit for finding the piles of leaves or urge him to pay more attention to following the mouse in front of him. Boss Mouse was a very good mouse. He never would belittle anyone, even if the reasons were justified.

XII
MIFFIT FINDS SHELTER

"It is time to stop for the evening," Boss Mouse told the group.

The family of mice was all grateful for the announcement. It had been a long day. It is not easy moving from one place to another like a mouse does. Their steps are very tiny and their tails drag, leaving dust for the mouse behind them. Often they have to miss a couple of meals that day, and it is not any fun traveling on empty stomachs. Miffit was always the first to notice the growls of hunger in his belly, and would begin asking when they could eat.

"I am hungry!" "I want something to drink", and "I am tired," were favorite phrases Miffit used each time they traveled from place to place.

Miffit spotted a couple small holes near the roots of the large acorn tree. He immediately ran to explore the possibilities for a night's lodging.

"It was perfect," he said in his squeaky voice, as he told the others in the group. "I think a squirrel has been living here," he suggested.

Boss Mouse asked him why he thought a squirrel had been living in the tree. "Because a bunch of acorn nuts are piled up near the trunk of the tree and squirrels like acorns."

Miffit knew that if these nuts had been stored for winter food by a squirrel he should not take any for himself. He had not forgotten the lesson from stealing the food from Gophie's house. Boss Mouse said all these nuts might have been gathered from the nuts that had fallen to the ground. Let us all begin searching the area under the tree to see if we can find enough for our meal tonight. Within a very few minutes the family of mice had found more than enough nuts to eat that evening. Boss Mouse knew that in the fall time of the year nuts from trees fall to the ground. It is nature's way to replenish old trees with young trees.

Boss Mouse told the group they could have some time for play in and under the leaves before it gets dark. It was a fun time for all the mice as they ran, jumped and scurried from pile to pile. This gave Boss Mouse time to plan and think about their final day of travel. He was worried about how to find the drooping eye turtle with the map on its stomach. How to avoid the imposters and not be gobbled up for a meal was something that bothered Boss Mouse a great deal. That was just the beginning of the issue. How does a mouse talk a turtle into turning upside down in able to read the map? Boss Mouse was creative and thorough, but how to read the map had temporarily stumped him. He realized that the mouse must see the underside of the turtle to read the map. When a turtle turns upside down, it becomes helpless, and often can never turn back over without assistance. How were they ever going to be able to read that map on the stomach of the turtle, and which turtle?

Mrs. Mouse suggested it might be time for eating their evening meal. Enough seeds and acorns had been gathered from under the leaves and grass for them to all be filled. Other young mice had found several tunnels and holes near the roots of the huge tree for sleeping that night. Boss Mouse told the group that early in the morning they would be leaving. He also said that within one more day they would reach the small stream where the drooping eyed turtle would be living. "It is important that none of us break away from the group tomorrow. Remember that Gophie told us about the imposters and how his great uncle never returned from his search of the map. The next day will be the most important one for us. Try to think about how to locate the drooping eyed turtle tonight when you go to sleep."

Boss Mouse worried most of the entire night about how to find the turtle with the map on its stomach. How did the map get there, and who put it there? He knew from experience that things are always better the next day. He learned not to worry about things that were not under his control anyhow. So, Boss Mouse put it out of his mind and would look forward to the new day. He had lots of responsibility in getting the entire family of mice across one more open area where they might easily be spotted by birds flying above or large rodents searching for food. He would need all the rest he could get that night, so off to sleep he drifted; at least for the moment.

Miffit yelled in his squeaky voice that someone was asking him "WHO, WHO, and WHO?" He was so scared of what type of creature may be talking to him in the middle of the night. It was unusual for Miffit to be awake so late but the full moon above made it nearly as bright as daytime. Then when he heard the 'WHO, WHO' calls, he yelled the loudest he could for anyone in the family to tell him what was taking place. Boss Mouse calmed Miffit down by telling him it was a wise old owl just talking to his family. Boss Mouse told Miffit to remain quiet and motionless because owls do their hunting at night. A favorite food for an owl is a mouse Miffit was told. "Close your eyes, do not move and go back to sleep. Things will all be better in the morning". Boss Mouse could make the worst things seem to be under control, and say the right words to calm all the mice when in times of deepest trouble.

After a restless night and less sleep than most of the family of mice wanted, it was time to begin the final day of the journey to find the drooping eyed turtle.   Boss Mouse hoped that the imposter would be easily recognized. Boss Mouse did not wish to sacrifice any of his family of mice for an imposter. He remembered Gophie told him to be cautious and watch out for imposters. "Why worry about something not within my control, Boss Mouse wondered. He would lead the family to the small stream and very cautiously watch and wait. He was confident that they would find the turtle with the map and then travel to the new land. "How exciting," he thought.

Miffit was curious about the turtle and the map on its stomach. He finally got enough courage to ask Boss Mouse if he understood how or why the map was on the stomach of the turtle. Boss Mouse reminded Miffit about his short whisker and how most of the mice would razz and tease him when he was young. Family members and friends often are cruel when it comes to poking fun at others that are somewhat different from the rest of the group. Generally, the one that looks a little out of place or is different from the others cannot help it. We need to be kind to those that are different. They can be special friends with unusual talents that may some day help you. It becomes a blessing to those in need when you are kind and generous. Boss Mouse continued to tell Miffit about the turtle with the drooping eye and how he eventually helped so many others.

"When the drooping eye turtle was hatched, do you remember that it scratched its eye on the eggshell? Many of the other turtles and small animals poked a lot of fun and jokes about the drooping eye. Often they would say "Oh your eye is blinking" or "Why does your eye look dumb and crooked". The daddy turtle wanted to change all the fun and teasing that had gone on about the drooping eye to an act of kindness. He worked very hard to use the markings on the drooping eye turtle as a map or guide to another place away from where they now lived. The daddy turtle told so few about the map that the drooping eye turtle became an extra special little fellow that was respected and loved by everyone. The markings on the little turtle's stomach seemed so important now that friends and family never even noticed the drooping eye. It was a very ingenious and clever method that drew attention from the obvious to the unnoticed and unrecognized." Miffit was so happy when he heard about that, that he had forgotten about his crooked tail and the one half- whisker. Boss Mouse was such a thoughtful and wonderful mouse. Miffit respected him more and more each day.

The family of mice had not traveled far when Boss Mouse noticed a reflection of the sun shining on water. He was sure that this must be the small stream they were looking for. It was going to be much easier for them once they found the stream and the drooping eye turtle. Boss Mouse had not yet figured out how to read the map under the stomach of the turtle, but was confident he would discover a method without hurting or harming the turtle. He was assured things would be so much easier in the new land with fresh seeds, grass to hide and play in, water to drink, and safe burrow to live and make their homes in. For now, he had to be content to find the stream and recognize the real drooping eye turtle, not the imposter.

XIII
OLD MOUSE GIVES WARNING

Several family members also recognized the glare on the water and yelled to Boss Mouse that the water was straight in front of them. So many questions, what do we do now? Where can we hide and be safe for a few hours?

"When can we eat?" asked Miffit.

Miffit was a young adult mouse now, who required a lot of food all the time. He could never get enough to eat, it seemed. Boss Mouse said they would only travel a little further.

He said, "I can see a small ravine near the stream of water. We can be safe there. We will gather some food for the night, find a place to stay and begin our search for the turtle. It will be necessary for us to have our scout mice find a place for the night near the ravine."

When the scout mice gave the 'all clear' sign to move forward, the entire mouse family began to travel to the ravine near the stream. Boss Mouse noticed an old white and gray mouse with only one ear slowly moving near by. When Boss Mouse shouted to the old mouse "Can we help you", the mouse paused for just a moment and looked around. It had poor eyesight and could not hear very well at all. Boss Mouse noticed that this old mouse was very skinny. It appeared to have not eaten for a few days.

With its aging voice, the old mouse responded, "Watch out for the imposter!"

Boss Mouse was curious now and very interested in what the old fellow had to say. Boss Mouse said they would gather some seeds for him to eat and protect him if he wanted. Boss Mouse asked the worker mice to find some fresh seeds for the old mouse to eat. The white and gray mouse was grateful for his newfound friends.

"Here is what happened," he said. "I had learned from another family that a turtle has a map on its stomach to a new and better land. I was told that the turtle with the map on the stomach would be different from all other turtles. I had spent hours and hours trying to find a turtle different from the others. All the markings seemed to look the same. Each one has a little tail, claws on their feet and a short little neck sticking out under their shell. It is so hard to see any difference with poor eyesight!" the old mouse stated.

"Then one day I saw a huge turtle sunning on the bank near the water. The more I watched and the closer I got, I noticed this old snapper would frequently blink its eyes. I do not remember the other turtles blinking their eyes often like the huge snapper, so my assumption was the snapper had the map on its stomach to the new land. I approached this giant turtle to ask about the map when he reached out with his long neck and bit my ear right off my head. I am glad that he only got my ear and not the rest of me, because he was a giant of a turtle. Ever since that day, I spend most of my time hiding."

Boss Mouse led the family into a safe area on the near bank of the ravine. They were in a position where they could see the stream in full view now. It was a safe place to spend the night and watch for the turtles coming to bask in the sun the following day. It would be very exciting, thought Miffit, as he began to search again for something to eat. He had been warned about wandering off alone just before dark in the past, but Miffit could only think about how to get his next meal. It was nearly dark now, but that did not bother Miffit. He thought he would not be caught or seen by anyone. After all, they are near water so that mean old ugly scruffy cat should not be in the area. Cats do not like water and stay away as far as they can from that stuff.

Boss Mouse asked that a meeting be planned so he could present to the colony, his plan on a couple of things that were on his mind. He knew that everyone wanted to know about how to find the drooping eye turtle and how to read the map on its stomach. Arrangements were made for the meeting to take place after the evening meal. Worker mice had been gathering more small grain, grass seeds and succulent water plant bulbs that had drifted to the bank. This was one of the better meals they had eaten since leaving Gophie's home. The entire family of mice agreed that life is good. Everyone was anxious to hear about the plan from Boss Mouse.

Following the dinner meal, Boss Mouse began the ritual of preparation for the meeting. He had not done this for several days now since they had been traveling and staying in different locations each night. He had carried along the special secret formula for his whiskers, and now was the time to use it. Cautiously and carefully, he applied the formula on the top two whiskers to make them bend upwards. They were shiny and bright and in the exact position. The bottom two whiskers had been combed and brushed with the formula to make them curve downward. The middle two whiskers stuck straight out from his face. He was very fond of his whiskers when they were in that position. It made him feel so important that decisions were easy to make. His thick grey and white fur had been brushed and brushed; making sure every hair was in its exact place. The meeting was about to begin, when in came Miffit.

Miffit arrived just about mid way during the evening meal. It became so quiet in the room when he stepped into the dining hall. Every eye was focused on Miffit. "What had he done this time," they thought! Miffit knew better than to make up any story or tell a lie about his whereabouts. He just made a decision to tell the truth, no matter how far fetched it might seem to be. Miffit said that he met another family of mice living in the area. They had a large family with some young girl mice who were trained as observers. They were known to have special skills in pointing out unusual things, and they shared some of their knowledge with Miffit!

XIV
MIFFIT READS THE MAP

Boss Mouse did not like to be interrupted any time during a meeting, especially one this important. It only took Boss Mouse one brief glance into the eyes of Miffit to let him know of his displeasure. Boss Mouse cleared his throat and said that Miffit was going to be responsible for learning how to read the map under the drooping eyed turtle. Everyone was shocked to hear what Boss Mouse had said. Boss Mouse always made every major decision that affected the lives of so many. This announcement was out of the ordinary, but now must be carried out. Boss Mouse was a wise leader with wisdom that amazed everyone. They all wondered how Miffit would make this important decision.

Miffit said that he was willing to make the decision on how to read the map under the belly of the drooping eye turtle. "Actually," he said, "I have been thinking about some possibilities that will not endanger or harm the turtle". Miffit said, "If we devise a method to turn the turtle upside down, it will be helpless and not able to turn back over again. So, that is not a good idea. I also thought that we could swim under the turtle in the water and read the map, but mice are horrible swimmers so that will not work." The entire group of mice was listening with both ears to what Miffit had to say. "Some of his ideas were good ones," a few of the mice commented.

Miffit offered several suggestions on finding the drooping eye turtle and reading the map on its stomach. After each idea was presented, someone always found reason why it would not work. "Oh, WOW, I have the perfect answer to reading the map Miffit offered. Listen to this idea" he said.

"Let us find some mud near the small stream," Miffit said. "Mud is easily found near the banks because the wind blows waves onto the dirt on the shore. The water soaks into the soil and then becomes mud. We will ask the drooping eye turtle to sit in the mud for a while until the mud dries. After the mud dries, the turtle can leave. When the turtle leaves the imprint of his stomach and the map will be left in the mud for us to use. We can follow the map to the new land. The map will show us the safe route from this side of the stream to the other side and the new and wonderful land. What do you think about that?" Miffit gloated.

For just an instant, silence was everywhere, not a sound from anyone. Then slowly sounds of encouragement came from numerous family members. Miffit had shown he had potential to be a leader and make decisions. He was wondering if he should be finding some of that secret formula for his 5 ½ whiskers too! His whiskers were not as long and ceremoniously elegant as Boss Mouse's whiskers, but he was proud of them nonetheless.

Before the recommendation and decision Miffit had made to the family of mice was initiated, Boss Mouse had to give the approving nod. Again all eyes were focused on the wise and ingenious leader. Boss Mouse gently cleared his throat, bobbed his head up and down for approval, and said, "We will use Miffit's plan tomorrow." I believe the plan is a wise plan, but I believe it may have one major flaw. I will reveal what I believe is the flaw after we have followed the map for a few hours. For now, let us all eat our evening meal, get some rest and prepare to find the drooping eyed turtle.

It was just daylight when most of the family members began to stir in their nesting places. They were all eager to get to the new land. They had heard through folklore about how the land had no cats or birds of prey. This was good news for the mouse family. Life would be so easy if they would not have to search for food a long distance from their burrows, and have water close by. To think of all the outside games they could play and not have to worry about cats chasing them. Miffit looked at the crook in his tail and thought he may forever be the last mouse in the land with a crook because there were no cats in the area.

"How wonderful, great, and enjoyable this new land was going to be!" Miffit said to himself. First of all the family of mice had to follow the map, cross the stream and get there. "Many things yet to do before the easy life," they all thought.

Boss Mouse said he wanted just a few scouts to travel to the stream banks in search of the drooping eyed turtle. Immediately, several volunteered for this adventure not knowing the eminent danger. Finding the real drooping eyed turtle would be a challenge. The imposter could be spotted more easily due to his size, and the possibility that his left eye may be the blinking one.

Within a few minutes after mid morning, the sun was brightly shining in the sky. Several turtles were basking on logs, clumps of grass and the banks near the shore. What a view these scouts were seeing as they peeped through the grass and gazed at the several turtles catching some sunrays. It was important for the scouts to search only for the drooping eyed turtle, not to think about the fun they could have playing near the water shore.

Unanimously they spotted the huge green snapper blinking its eye. Sure enough, it was the left eye that was drooping and blinking. An old ugly rat approached the imposter, apparently for information about the map. Closer and closer the rat came to the turtle, slowly and cautiously watching every blink and droop of the eye. The rat was not expecting what took place next! The old snapper in a mysterious way nodded for the rat to come just a little bit closer to him, as his hearing was not so good he said. Rats are known for their cunningness and keen ability to survive in all circumstances. In less time than it takes to make two blinks of an eye, the snapper lunged forward and bit off a huge chunk of the rats'

tail. That SNAP was heard way out where the scouts were hiding. It was a lesson the mice viewed first hand that they did not want to learn from experience like the rat. The scouts talked amongst themselves for a few seconds before they reported the findings back to Boss Mouse.

Boss Mouse listened eagerly to what the scouts had to say. He asked the scouts if they could notice any difference in the turtles from where they were hiding. They did notice that the snapper was somewhat larger than all the others were and remained further from the shore. "We will observe the turtles that are close to shore or on logs sunning themselves from now on, and stay away from that old ugly imposter." With that, the scouts went out again that afternoon to find the drooping eyed turtle.

They had only been looking for a very few minutes when they noticed a medium sized painted turtle crawl out of the water on to the bank. The turtle had its back to the mice making it difficult for them to catch a glimpse of the eye of the turtle. The scouts had to move to a new position, so they did so very quickly without disturbing the basking turtle. When they were in a good position where they could see both the painted turtle's eyes, they glared intensely at this turtle, hoping this was the one they had been looking for. In a few seconds, the right eye of the turtle began to droop and blink rapidly. The scouts were so pleased to think they had found the turtle on only their second try. They were so anxious to tell Boss Mouse about what they had seen. The scouts had never made it back to the mouse family so quickly!

Boss Mouse told the group, "Now we must bargain with the turtle for the information on its stomach".

Boss Mouse was sure the turtle had been approached before for information about the map so it would not propose any problem he thought.

"We will have to just ask for cooperation from the turtle to let us read the map," Boss Mouse said.

Miffit's plan of letting the turtle set in the mud to get the imprint will work. We will offer the turtle its favorite food for the evening meal, for setting in the mud. In addition, we can act as watchdogs protecting it from an approaching enemy while making the imprint for us.

Boss Mouse was such a good leader. His advice was thoughtful and sensible. 'Leaders that are fair will last a long time, just as Boss Mouse has done.' He was highly respected and well liked through out the entire mouse family.

The following afternoon the sun was very high in the sky and quite hot for this time of the year. It was an excellent day for drying imprints in the mud on the bank next to the shore. The wind had blown early in the day making little mud puddles along the bank of the stream.

Lucky for the mouse family, the drooping eyed painted turtle chose some mud to sit in and sun himself for a few minutes. He could have selected a log or clump of grass like some of the other turtles did that afternoon. The mouse family would have to remain quiet and sit still until the sun dried the mud under the turtle. It seemed like a very long wait, but when someone is anxious, it seems much longer than it really is. That was the case this afternoon. Soon enough the sun went under the clouds and the turtle slithered back to the safety of the water. Boss Mouse signaled to Miffit to come and memorize the impression so they could use it for travel tomorrow morning. Miffit and several others had committed the map to memory and would start their journey to the new land tomorrow-early morning. Boss Mouse urged Miffit to think very hard about the decision to follow the map.

He said, "The entire family of mice is depending on your leadership tomorrow."

XV
MIFFIT LEADS THE GROUP THE WRONG WAY

Finally, Miffit had the chance of his lifetime to stay out of mischief and do something good for once. Even Miffit himself with his 5 1/2 whiskers, doubted if he could focus totally on how to save the mouse family, rather than have fun and play games. He had spent sufficient time in looking at the imprint in the mud the drooping eye turtle had left. He, along with several others, had discussed the route to take to the new land. It was an exciting time for the family of mice. Miffit had even forgotten to think about food on this morning, and that was most unusual for him. No matter how important the mission or responsibility, Miffit would have drifted off course to find a game to play and some new food to try eating. All the mice had taken their place in line in preparation for the move to the new land. It would be different this time, because Boss Mouse would follow Miffit.

"The map pointed in this direction," Miffit said. "We travel the very same way as our last move, so let us get going."

All the family of mice had done this many times before so they knew the drill of who follows who and knowing the mouse in front and behind them. Miffit led the family in a Westerly direction toward the setting sun. He remembered from the map that soon they would see a grove of trees used as a shelterbelt. Tall grass to the North, he remembered, with a ravine crossing South East from the trail they were to follow. Miffit did not notice by the map that the field they crossed was full of sand burrs and weeds with thorns. Why, only after a few hours, they were out of sight of each other because of the dense thicket and briars causing some to lose their place. Others were stopping to remove stickers that were caught in their fur, which was further delaying the journey to the new land. "It was not supposed to be like this," Miffit thought to himself! They should not have to travel in weeds and thorns to find the new land. Gophie had not told them anything about a difficult journey. Miffit began to doubt that he was leading the family in the correct direction. Should he call on Boss Mouse for guidance? "How much further should I go?" he wondered.

In addition, the weather was very hot with a humid wind causing the entire family to become thirstier than ever. With no water in sight and not able to carry water, the family of mice was close to a disaster. Miffit wished at this point that he had not elected to lead the family of mice to the new land. He could hear complaints from several mice with sand burr stickers in their fur. Others were griping about no water and how hot it was that day. Reluctantly, Miffit was forced to ask for the help of the capable leader, Boss Mouse.

"I am confused and bewildered," Miffit explained to Boss Mouse.

XVI
BOSS MOUSE READS THE MAP

"What should I do now?" Miffit asked Boss Mouse. Miffit knew that an answer from Boss Mouse would be the right one, getting the mouse family on track again. Just after a few hours, Miffit felt that he was not going to be a good leader. He was much better at finding things to play with and avoiding any kind of work.

"I am willing to help you in any way I can," Boss Mouse told Miffit.

Boss Mouse asked the mouse family to return to the location where the imprint had been left in the mud by the drooping eye turtle. All the mice wondered just why they were returning to look again at the map in the mud from the imprint. Without hesitation, the mouse family was led to the imprint in the mud by Miffit and a couple scouts. It was easy to find since it had only been one full day since the drooping eyed turtle left the impression in the mud along the bank.

"Now let us examine the map more closely," said Boss Mouse. "You notice that the arrow guiding us through the grove of trees and just North of the ravine is pointing in the direction of where the turtle's head is. Boss Mouse further explained to the group of mice that Miffit had done a good job of leading the family according to the directions in the mud, but overlooked one major detail.

"Does anyone know why we were led in the wrong direction through the sand burrs and thorns, making travel difficult?" asked

Boss Mouse. "Notice that on the map clumps of grass show shallow puddles of water near by. This water can be used for our travel, but we did not see any water."

"Does anyone have a clue or suggestion as to why we went the wrong direction?" Boss Mouse asked.

Mrs. Mouse thought she knew the answer but opted not to say a thing. She was known for having few words, but when she spoke everyone paid attention. This time she was not going to speak. A couple of the scouts offered a suggestion or two about why they went the wrong direction, but the correct answer eluded them. After a few moments and many suggestions on why they had gone the wrong direction, Boss Mouse began to clear his throat. They all knew this was the signal to listen and pay attention. Boss Mouse opted to reveal his decision after he had conducted the ritual and applied the secret formula on the six whiskers, of which he was extremely proud.

Everyone wondered just how the ritual could be shortened this time, as they were very anxious to get the answer. To their surprise, Boss Mouse told the group it would not be necessary to complete the entire ritual today.

"The decision I will make is very important to our entire family and our freedom from where we now live" Boss Mouse began. "We all want to be able to work and play without watching for cats and predators. So, you two mice brushing my fur, only do it one time, which will suffice for now. I will only apply a small amount of secret formula on my whiskers to speed up the process." After his fur had been combed in a hurry and two whiskers pointing up, two down and the middle two straight out, Boss Mouse was ready to give the decision.

"It was a good lesson learned today," Boss Mouse said. "Miffit and the two scouts paid attention to detail, but overlooked the obvious solution and had jumped to conclusions. Plans and decisions made under hasty conditions cannot compare to well thought out and deliberate ones," Boss Mouse said. "The plan Miffit offered to us was incorrect because he overlooked the simple answer."

"When you look at an impression in the mud from the underside of a turtle, did you realize the image must be reversed?" Boss Mouse explained.

Miffit and the scouts were looking and thinking the map directions had to be followed exactly the way it appeared in the mud from the impression on the turtle's stomach. The lesson to learn from this mistake is that when using an impression for directions, you must reverse the images making all directions opposite of what you see in the mud. So in this case, notice that the arrow indicated to travel

North by Northwest. In reality, you must go in the opposite direction to arrive at the new land told to us about by Gophie. The ravine will be west of us now, not east as Miffit and the scouts had thought. Now when we leave in the morning we can use the illustrations on the map, but go the other direction and we will reach the new land.

Miffit was again amazed with the wisdom Boss Mouse seemed to always have, and at the precise moment. Had the mouse family all listened to Miffit they would all be stuck with sandburs, cockleburs, and thorns. Going without any water in scorching sun and nothing to eat was life threatening to the family of mice also. Miffit was pleased that Boss Mouse had not humiliated or belittled him because of his detrimental leadership qualities. One day Miffit hoped to be as polite and graceful with his decisions as was Boss Mouse. It was very difficult to provide probable options when the mouse family had been led in the wrong direction and gone without food or water for a day. Boss Mouse's wise decisions were based on understanding and his life-long, far-reaching background. He was a kind and thoughtful leader loved by all and respected by everyone. Boss Mouse was an expert at making everyone feel good, even though his or her advice might be incorrect or inaccurate. Miffit was pleased that Boss Mouse had helped him out of another dilemma.

Tomorrow arrived, finally, after the evening games had been played. Miffit, even though he was a young adult now, still enjoyed playing more than working. Boss Mouse wondered if he would ever grow up and be responsible to anyone other than himself. It takes a lot of time to develop character traits that Boss Mouse taught the mouse family. "Miffit cannot be so full of mischief and want to play all his life," Boss Mouse thought to himself. "Perhaps when we get to the new land Miffit will work finding food and water to drink rather than seeking pleasure."

"Well, we must travel according to the map directions," Boss Mouse stated to the assembled group. "The arrow points toward the rising sun with the ravine to the South. We will travel as before - I lead, then Miffit and Mrs. Mouse follow, then all others in the line. I believe we can find berries and seeds along the way now," Boss Mouse said. "Fall time is here so farmers have spilled seeds on the ground during their hauling loads to the storage bins. This time of the year, we can expect to see lots of ripe berries and fruits on the bushes and small trees. It will not be difficult for us to find and eat the food when it is ripe and ready for harvest," Boss Mouse said. "Fruit and berries, when ripe, fall off their vines and branches so we can eat the things on the ground. And when the wind blows it helps us," Boss Mouse said, "because ripe fruit falls easily off the vines." Follow Me," Boss Mouse shouted to the family of mice.

Miffit asked Boss Mouse how they were going to cross the small stream.

"I have a couple of ideas," Miffit said. "Do you want to hear some of them?"

Boss Mouse was more interested in traveling now, than listening to another idea that might result in total failure. Boss Mouse had a lot on his mind this day, and one thing was not more hair-brained thoughts from immature mice. Boss Mouse told the group that within a few hours they should be able to see the shallow ditches and short trees that they had seen on the map of the turtle.

"About noon time, we can pause for fresh fruit and berries and think about specific directions for our afternoon traveling."

They were all so pleased that everything was going so well for them. Boss Mouse was a very special mouse to the entire mouse family. No one was ever disrespectful or talked behind his back, clearly a wonderful leader that always thought of the family of mice before he thought of himself.

XVII
UNDERGROUND TUNNELS WITH
PRAIRIE DOGS

    Miffit was willing to make suggestions to Boss Mouse on how to cross over the small stream to the new land. He had been thinking all day about some, what he thought were very clever ideas on how to cross the stream. He suggested to Boss Mouse that they should find a beaver who could cut down a tree, making a bridge over the stream. Another thought he had was to use some dry leaves that had fallen from the tree as a little boat to float across the shallow stream. Still he thought about just swimming under water holding your breath crossing to the other side. Boss Mouse gave Miffit one of those glares of bewilderment as the suggestions were made to him.

    Boss Mouse said he had known many athletic mice that could accomplish wonderful things, but swimming under water was not one of them. When the fur on a mouse gets soaked with water, it becomes so heavy it weighs the mouse down keeping it from further swimming. Since the stream is flowing slowly, it is nearly impossible to float on a leaf from one side to the other without winding up not where you intended to be.

    "If you get to the wrong place on the other side, you can become lost and confused. I think you all know that if a tree forms a bridge over the stream for us to walk on, then other animals can cross on the same bridge too. So if we cross on the tree bridge, then mean old ugly cats also can come across." Boss Mouse said he had the best plan of all. "Please listen to it, "he told the mouse family."

"Can you remember several days ago while traveling, we met some other cousins of ours?" said Boss Mouse. "You may remember we met larger cousins called prairie dogs and gophers. Gophers and prairie dogs use elaborate underground tunnels for their homes, traveling from place to place and storing food. Gophie told us about how to find the turtle with the map and about the new land, when we were sleeping in his home that night. Did any of you notice how many choices of tunnels you could choose from to travel into that night? Some of those underground burrows went in all directions and at various lengths and depths. We want to choose a hole that is large enough to allow passage and safe travel yet small enough so that any ugly old furry cats cannot follow us."

"I believe we can find a colony of gophers near the small stream that might be familiar with the new land. The map on the stomach of the turtle will lead us to the small grove of trees near the stream. It will be at that place where both gophers and prairie dogs live. They can find nuts from the trees to eat, berries from the bushes that grow in the moist soil near the banks of the stream, so they will live very near by. It would be better for us to use tunnels made by the gophers for our travel to the new land."

"We can gnaw on and eat roots that grow underground in the tunnels. Since water runs down hill and settles in the lowest points, we can find water at the very bottom of the tunnels. Our cousins, the gophers, are gregarious rodents. We can find the colony next to the stream and tell them we have been directed by Gophie. Some member of that group just might be a relative or have heard about Gophie and let us use their tunnel to pass under the stream to the other side. It will be tricky to know which way to travel since it is always dark in the tunnel and there are so many from which to choose. It will be necessary to use our instinct to meander through the maze of tunnels and burrows, finding our way to the other side of the stream."

"These cousins have dug deep enough below the water level of the stream that their tunnel will pass under the water and up on the other side. They will have to make it difficult to find so that just not anyone can get to the new land. Gophie did tell us how to get to the edge of the stream, but not beyond. Perhaps we will be able to travel below the water in the stream safely and reach the other side." Boss Mouse said he would have to think very hard about how to find his way in underground tunnels. He had not done this before, but was sure he could figure it out. Miffit suggested that when under ground they could put their ears to the soil and be able to hear the water rushing over the gravel and rocks above.

"WHAT DID YOU SAY?" said Boss Mouse! "That is an absolutely excellent idea to be able to tell which way to go! Remember visiting with the mouse with only one ear? This makes me think," said Boss Mouse.

"I just wonder if that old mouse had put its ear to the soil trying to hear the water above so many times the ear had worn off. When we were visiting with the old mouse with one ear, he told me about using the ear to find directions. At that time, I was unclear about what he was saying and understanding the reason of putting the ear to the soil. It makes more sense now," Boss Mouse said.

"When I was a very young mouse, my dad would put his ear to the ground during early morning and evening before we would go out and search for berries and nuts to eat. I guess I never did ask him why he was doing that, but now understand that he was listening for vibrations and sounds on the ground. If he could feel the vibrations or hear sounds, it meant that animals or larger rodents were close by, and would not allow us to go in search of food until no sounds were heard. My father was a very clever mouse," Boss Mouse said.

"And that old one-eared mouse used that trick so many times to save his life, and leads others to the new and better land. We are fortunate we met that old mouse that day. We will use our ears to guide us below and across the stream into the new land."

It was only a very short time when they had noticed a large number of holes in the ground near the short trees and bushes. It was exactly like the map had shown under the turtle - short trees and small bushes near the stream, where many gopher and prairie dog holes would be visible. Boss Mouse was sure pleased to know they had followed the map directions getting them to this place. All the family of mice had grown tired by this time of the day. Of course, Miffit was ready to have some fun and eat some food. Food was in good supply here because of the moist soil, dense vegetation and a long way from where the farmers could harvest. Boss Mouse thought it might be time for a celebration, and that is what the family did for the next few hours before they were off to sleep.

So many choices of lush berries and nuts had fallen from the trees, and there was fresh water to drink. They all were hungry and thirsty, so thoroughly enjoyed eating to their fill on snacks and treats they had not eaten in several days. Everyone was happy! Even the prairie dogs knew they were going to protect their cousins as they traveled to the new land. What a wonderful time it was for the mouse family today. Tomorrow they would be in search of the right tunnel under the stream to the new land.

Many of the mice had begun to question Boss Mouse about what they could expect to find in the new land. Their minds were wandering with amazement and anticipation, just thinking about how great it might be. Miffit thought about how he could play all day and never work again. Mrs. Mouse hoped she could have a little larger tunnel to live in that might be closer to water. Still others wondered if they could be free of cats or other animals that hunt mice. Boss Mouse told the group he would respond to all their questions early in the morning before they began to cross under the stream. Some of the mouse family did not sleep very soundly that night because they were thinking too hard about what would happen next.

Boss Mouse was a discerning and clever mouse with more experience than any other mouse in the entire family. The group waited, but not patiently, to hear the answers Boss Mouse was going to share with them. Since this might be the last meeting before Boss Mouse considered relinquishing his authority and responsibility, he opted to share a couple of life-long, tightly held secrets to selected members of the mouse family. Everyone sat very quietly in their appointed positions on the very edge of their seat while Boss Mouse cleared his throat and began to speak.

Of course, his whiskers were precisely positioned; two curved up, two down and the other two straight out. They glistened and shown so brightly that they reflected light just like a mirror. Many of the more maturing mice hoped they would be selected as the successor to lead the mouse family like Boss Mouse had done so well for many years.

Boss Mouse began speaking distinctly and slowly to the group.

"I have decided to share my governing duties with some younger maturing mice from our large family of mice," Boss Mouse stated. "The decision to give up part of the decision making process is a difficult one," he said. "We must have a leader that leads by example, not self serving, and one who cares for others at all times." "Since this is such an important process I will ask some of you for suggestions on choosing the next leader".

XVIII
MIFFIT CAUGHT IN A WHIRLWIND

Miffit wanted to be the next leader, but knew that his immaturity and foolishness would not get him appointed to the leadership responsibility. He decided that he would slip outside of the meeting place and search for something extra to eat for a late night snack. He soon found a container less than one-half filled with sunflower pits that looked so very inviting. He wanted to sample some of those sunflower pits so badly that his stomach began to growl. It was so loud that he wondered if the other mice would hear the noise and begin looking for him.

It was the season of very high winds and blowing dust, as it had been dry this past season. Boss Mouse had instructed the entire the colony on protective measures during the windy parts of the year. Of course, Miffit, like during all other meetings, had been thinking about something else during the training period. This was not unusual for Miffit to act like this, but unfortunately, this time he missed very important life saving steps that Boss Mouse had given to the group.

At the precise moment, Miffit began to taste his first sunflower pit, a whirlwind swept through the area. The only one in danger was Miffit because he was again, not listening to the important decisions being made by Boss Mouse. Boss Mouse could feel in his bones drastic weather changes and severe climatic differences. Often times Boss Mouse would know a few hours in advance of radical weather changes due to the way he felt. Boss Mouse said it was difficult to explain and hard to understand, but he could predict high wind, blowing dust, and moisture in the air all due to aching joints and stiffening muscles. Boss Mouse many times in past years had rescued and saved the colony from disaster by giving them advance warning of sudden weather changes that would put the colony at risk or danger.

Miffit was always worried about his stomach, and any warning of wind or storm was not going to stop him from having another snack. So he began to gnaw and chew on those tasty sunflower pits. He was dining on the rare treat he had found when the whirlwind swept through the area without any warning. Boss Mouse had felt in his bones a severe change taking place, but was overcome with thoughts of selecting his own replenishment, that he neglected to inform any others. After all, why should he worry? Everyone was at the meeting and protected from wind or rain, at least for the moment. But wait, where was Miffit?!!

The whirlwind whipped in and around and was gone before anyone could try to find Miffit. The whirlwind sucked up everything in its path as it passed through the area that evening. Miffit was inside the container of sunflower pits as the wind whirled, twisted and formed a cloud of dust and debris from everything gathered from the surrounding area. This storm, like many others, had arrived quickly and without warning. Miffit was taking the ride of his life in the sunflower pit container, as the whirlwind had unwillingly relocated Miffit to a very unfamiliar place!!! This was one time that Miffit had wished he had not opted for a late night snack.

Truly Miffit was afraid, lonely and without friends or family members for support during times when needed most.

"What am I going to do?" he wondered.

He began to reflect on past teachings from his leader Boss Mouse.

"Where am I, and how did I get here?" He last remembered dining on sunflower pits and being near the colony of mice that offered security and safety. Oh, how he wanted to be back under the protection and guidance of Boss Mouse! Miffit was nearly overwhelmed with sadness as he began to think his way out of the predicament he found himself in.

Miffit could hear talking, but unable to understand what was said. Perhaps it was because they were too far away or their voices were muffled by the loud music and sound from the busyness of numerous activities that were unfamiliar to him. Miffit began to follow the unfamiliar sounds of talking to get a closer look at just where they might be coming from. He was led into a dark dank huge hole near a smaller oak tree at the North end of the area. He could clearly hear from outside the hole near the tree, yet did not understand what everyone was saying. "How can I be so confused?" he thought.

Miffit was drawn closer to the group of mice from the laughter and sounds of cheering that were taking place. He was not sure what they were doing, but interested enough to ask one member of the group if he could join them, as he was very much alone and afraid. When Miffit spoke to the group of mice, they acted as if they did not understand what he was saying. It was then Miffit knew these mice were speaking another language with which he was not familiar. He knew that this was some place he had never been, and from what he had seen thus far did not want to stay there very long! He was further withdrawn from the group, and sadly left trying to find his way back to his friends and the security of Boss Mouse.

XIX
MIFFIT IS LOST AND CONFUSED

After wandering aimlessly most of the night, Miffit found himself totally lost, really hungry, and missing the comforts of his family group of mice. Oh, how he longed to sit in a meeting where Boss Mouse would give wise counsel and guidance for the next day's events. Miffit knew that he must get back to the family group! But, how?

Later on that afternoon, he noticed an older teenaged brownish mouse that just seemed so 'cool'. This young fellow was an upscale and inquisitive guy who seemed to know the ropes of coping with life, no matter what circumstances you might find yourself in. Miffit listened with interest and supportive energy to what this young guy was telling him. And, Miffit could *not* understand, because they were speaking a different language. "That foreign stuff being spoken last night was Spanish," Miffit was told. "You are now in another region of the country and English is not understood by everyone here."

Miffit wanted to act and look cool like this newfound friend; or at least Miffit thought this guy was a new and good friend. Miffit was coached into getting an ear pierced, to be with the trend and look of this new location. Miffit was so gullible that he did get an ear pierced, but not without consequences. Since the shop had been so busy with customers that day, Miffit was rushed in and out without proper preparation. His ear became sore and slightly swollen from the rushed job. Miffit learned one quick lesson that afternoon about new friends and their unfounded thoughts and ideas. It would be a lesson he would long remember.

Starting out hungry and with a lousy friendship just ended, is not the best way to begin finding your way back to where the whirlwind had picked you up! What seemed like forever that day, was only a few hours before Miffit found something to eat beneath a huge full-grown acorn tree. Acorns can provide sufficient nourishment for nearly one day for a small mouse, but getting them open can be very difficult. Miffit was surrounded with food to eat, but the covering over the nut inside the shell was too difficult to crack, so he was still

hungry. He tried over, and over again to crack the acorn nut, but just did not have the strength in his jaws to crack that nut.

As evening approached, a two-horned owl landed in the tree to look over the area in search of food. Mice are favorite foods for owls. Boss Mouse had trained Miffit in the past about keeping out of sight of owls. This time Miffit hoped it would be different. Perhaps if Miffit pointed out all the acorns the owl could eat, it would take its mind off eating a fresh mouse. Miffit told the owl that many acorns were on the ground and very good to eat. "I am having a great amount of difficulty in cracking these things, could you help me?" Miffit asked the owl. "You have a very strong beak that could break open these nuts and have a fine meal".

The two-horned owl looked down on Miffit with one eye at a time, thinking about making a choice between one mouse or many nuts to eat.

"Where are you trying to go?" asked the owl. Miffit told him he was lost and trying to get back to the colony of mice, led by their leader, Boss Mouse.

"I am not familiar with who Boss Mouse is, but do know where a family of mice live in a new land," the owl told Miffit. "I can help you get back to that area, but it will require a few days journey" the owl told Miffit.

"How do I know that I can trust you?" Miffit ask the two-horned owl.

"You were kind to me by sharing your food supply," the owl said. "I will be repeating that act of kindness by using my wings to help you rejoin your lost family." "Doing acts of kindness for one another benefits everyone," the owl said.

Miffit wondered just when he could begin the journey and how he would be guided. It was time to take a rest, but not easy to sleep on an empty stomach. Miffit had to settle for a few not-so-tasty grass seeds before crawling under some acorn leaves to go to sleep that evening.

When the Eastern sun came up the next morning, the two-horned owl was gone. Miffit again was alone, and more worried than the night before. He observed birds soaring in the sky above, circling lower and lower. Miffit had remembered Boss Mouse instructing the colony to be aware of flat flying birds. These are birds that fly, float and soar through the air without flapping their wings. Their wings are straight out from their body, flat like a pancake.

Beware of these birds of prey, they will swoop down and catch a mouse like a bolt of lightening from the sky. Beware! Beware! Is all Miffit could think about as he watched these flat flyers from under the acorn leaf.

Miffit began to move from the safety of the huge acorn tree, traveling with the sun behind him. He thought this would be the best way because the sun would cast a shadow over him and hide him from the birds of prey.

He had not been going very long when he heard some one say, "Go West, Go West". It was the owl. Miffit was so pleased to be given some direction in which way to travel. The owl had returned from its parliament (a parliament is what a group of owls is called) and pledged an act of kindness to Miffit. The owl told Miffit to follow red- bellied and red-breasted birds.

"They are your friends. You know, like robins or nuthatches. Boss Mouse and the colony lives to the West, so just use the red-bellied birds as your guide."

Miffit was well on his way to finding his former colony of mice when he noticed the sun's reflection in the immediate distance to the North of where he had been traveling.

"What is causing the reflection?" he wondered. "How could there be any reflection when all you can see is sand and piles of sand blown and shaped by the wind?" Miffit could see the flat flyers overhead, but heard coaxing and chirping from the red-bellied birds that beckoned and called him to follow them. The two- horned owl had been right! Follow the red-breasted flyers and take guidance from them and they will lead you in a westerly direction. The further he moved in a westerly direction the more and more he could see the glare off to the North. "What is that shiny thing?" Miffit wondered.

After traveling a little longer, Miffit was close enough to have a closer look at what was causing the reflection he had been observing. He had never seen any animal or bird that was pure white like new fallen snow. The sun was being reflected from a very tiny pure white animal.

"What is this?" Miffit wondered. He slowly moved in the direction of the reflection, being ever so cautious not to disturb or alarm this beautiful little creature. "Could I converse with it, or should I totally ignore it and travel on?"

It was nearly dark by the time Miffit raised enough courage to approach the white shiny animal. This creature was so white and beautiful, that it could be seen in the darkness, Miffit realized. He had viewed the owl in the darkness before, but that was because the moonlight had cast enough light for the owl to be seen sitting in the tree branches. This little white and shinny animal was easily recognized in total darkness. Miffit opted to think more about it later as he found a couple of old branches and bushes blown against a huge pile of sand where he would sleep and rest for the night.

XX
MIFFIT AND ANDSHE MEET

The next morning the sun was shining brightly. There were no clouds in the sky and only a little breeze was blowing the sand piles around. Miffit awoke early remembering that he was trying to find this shiny white animal. In the heavy damp morning air, Miffit could smell something he had never experienced before. It was not that of green leaves or fresh berries or nuts on which to eat. The smell was like ground up rose pedals or squished pink or lavender flowers from lush plants.

"Wow! This was a new experience," Miffit thought." He decided to follow this pleasant scent and see what was producing such a fragrant and delightful smell. Miffit had never experienced anything like this.

Miffit and all the other mice in the colony were grey in color with a tint of faint brown or white. There were no pure white mice in any colony Miffit had ever known or met.

"This lily-white animal could not be a mouse, could it?"

Miffit was the one to speak first to this pure white animal. "Can you help me?" Miffit asked this little creature.

"Hi" was the response.

Miffit continued to introduce himself, explaining his predicament and the reasons why he was trying to get back to the Boss Mouse colony. The little white creature was friendly and interested in what

Miffit had been telling her. Miffit was mystified to learn that this beautiful little pure white creature was a mouse, also.

"Where I live here in this very hot and humid region, most of the mice are white in color," she told Miffit. "We are fair and light colored to reflect the hot sun, helping to keep us cool during the seasonable warm months. My family and I live above ground in abandoned piles of wood. My family and I are factory workers. We have little time to hunt for food or play mousy games.

"I am named Andshe," she told Miffit. "My parents call me Andshe, because they say; *and she* can work hard, *and she* can run fast, *and she* is also beautiful. "What is your name and how did you get it?" she asked Miffit.

Miffit could not remember how he got his name, but remembered that he was just getting out of or into trouble most of the time. Miffit told Andshe about his family, and why he was trying to get back to the new land.

"It has been a long and tiring journey," he told Andshe.

"Oh, how were you able to spot or find me?" she asked Miffit.

"I first noticed a bright reflection from the sun on your pure white fur. But what really led me to find you was that smell of chewed flowers." "Why do you smell like that?" Miffit asked her.

"Oh, it is girl thing and you would not understand." Andshe said. "Do you have any plans or can you stay here for awhile?"

Miffit explained that he was trying very hard to get back under the safety and guidance of Boss Mouse. He had been traveling for a while alone now and sure could use some help in locating the new land where his family was.

"Are you interested in traveling with me and assisting me with getting back home?"

Andshe was usually quiet and could hold back her emotions, but this time it was different. Immediately, perhaps even prematurely and full of excitement she responded with, "Yes! I will travel with you!"

Andshe said they could remain in her home for the night, dine on some good seeds and nuts that evening, before starting their journey tomorrow. Miffit was so pleased that AndShe would join him for the return back to the colony. He was happy to have a companion that could share and assist in making decisions on how to return to the new land. Tomorrow could not come soon enough, Miffit thought. He hardly slept that night, thinking of how wonderful it was going to be with his new friend, Andshe, traveling together.

After saying good-bye to her family, Andshe and Miffit began their journey to the West in search of the new land. They had not been traveling very long before the red bellied fliers circled just above their heads. Andshe was frightened, but Miffit assured her that the two-horned owl had requested following only the red-bellied flyers. Miffit told Andshe that the rest-breasted fliers would guide them in a Westerly direction. "When we observe their circling above, follow their lead. Beware of those flat flying birds. They are the ones that will swoop down, grab you with their claws, and take you away. If you see those flat flyers, be sure to take immediate cover for your life!"

They had been traveling for only the first morning when Andshe wondered when they would find something to eat. She had always had prepared meals, and regularly scheduled because of the hours she spent working at the textile factory. Miffit had not experienced that routine before, whenever he found food, he began eating. He was never sure when the next meal was going to take place, so "Eat when you can," he figured.

"By the way, what is a textile factory?" he asked Andshe.

"My family and I work making shirts and shorts for mice who want to dress and wear fashionable styles," Andshe told Miffit. "We are in an area where many mice live very close to each other. When all the mice are white in color, the same size and all look quite the same, it becomes very difficult to tell one from the other. My family began making shirts and shorts of different colors to be worn by family members so we could tell one from another. The colors I wear are bright red and light pink," she said.

"Most of the boys wear blue and tan colors. That way we can easily recognize family members and boys and girls from a distance," Andshe said.

Miffit told Andshe he thought it would be dangerous wearing bright colored shirts or shorts where he lived, because cats and birds recognize bright colors and could easily prey upon members of the mouse family. He lived in open areas where highflying birds would circle above looking to catch a mouse for their lunch. Mice wearing bright colors could easily catch the eye of birds flying above.

Andshe said, "They did not have too worry about that sort of thing since most of the time they lived and worked in buildings that were covered. "

"Hey, we had better get to following those red- bellied flyers," Miffit said. "They have been circling and circling, showing us that we need to be heading west."

They had not traveled very long after Miffit realized he should try to send Boss Mouse a message letting him know he was on his way back to the colony.

"How can a mouse send a message?" Miffit wondered. He had shared this dilemma with his friend Andshe, and hoped that she would have a couple of suggestions on sending a message to Boss Mouse. "Andshe was clever and creative," Miffit had thought, so just maybe she could give him an idea that would work.

"Do you have any idea or way we could send a message to Boss Mouse?" asked Miffit.

"I have an idea that might work in sending a message," she told Miffit.

Some time ago during Andshe's younger and adventurous ways, she had been playing in an area that was being over run with her larger cousins, brown and gray rats. Even though she knew better, curiosity overcame her and she adventured into the rat-infested area. She had never seen a rat trap before and was surprised to find out from her own mistake, that they can do permanent damage to your claws when they SNAP shut. Andshe had been caught in one of those traps by her pinky. Her claw nail instantly turned dark green, light gray and black. What seemed like a long time later her pinky nail grew back pure white, much like the color and hardness of tusks on elephants.

XXI
ANDSHE'S PINKY REFLECTS A MESSAGE

"All my nails are colored pink and red using drops of juice from ripe berries and red pedals of rose bushes," Andshe told Miffit.

"These squeezed fruits and flowers are so easy to use in coloring my claw nails, but do not have any effect on my white tusk-like nail," she said. "I often use my white nail as a mirror when combing my hair," Andshe told Miffit. "I can see my own reflection in this pure white nail, and also I have noticed when brightly shining sun shines on my nail, the glare is seen some place else".

"Perhaps we could use your nail to send signals or messages," said Miffit. "Let us give it a try".

Miffit pointed to a rock covered with mica off to the West that he thought could be used as a reflection point. Miffit had noticed that when the sun shines on mica rocks it does cause a bright glare.

"The reflective glare catches your attention during times when the sun shines brightly. Today the sun is shining very brightly," Miffit told

Andshe. "We will not be able to send our reflection message when the sun is under a cloud or during rainy days." "Can we try to send the message today?" Andshe asked Miffit.

We must think of what message to send Boss Mouse," Miffit suggested to Andshe.

"Our message must be brief and important," Miffit said.

It would be much easier if we could send letters using all straight lines and no round or curved letters, Andshe thought.

"Let us see now, what types of letters use straight lines?" Miffit wondered. He began thinking of straight-line letters; X or L, maybe a Z, but not R or S because letters with curves would not make the proper reflection. Since the mica rock is small, only three letters could be sent as a message to Boss Mouse.

"I sure wish Boss Mouse could be here," Miffit thought. Boss Mouse always had wise and important answers to all the problems the mouse colony ever had. Boss Mouse was not here to help; Miffit and Andshe had to create their own message using only three letters.

"Hold your claw nail like this" Miffit said as he described the way Andshe should use her claw nail to reflect the sun on the mica rock in the distance. "When you move your nail up down and sideways as the sun shines, the reflection can make a letter on the mica rock," Miffit said. "Let us try and send a straight line letter first," he said.

Andshe pointed her nail toward the brightly shinning sun as she followed the directions given by Miffit. "Be sure to point exactly toward the shiny mica rock," Miffit told Andshe. It was difficult at first to reflect the sun from her claw nail to the shiny mica rock off in the distance. After trying a few times, Andshe had learned how to move her claw back and forth to form reflecting letters on the shiny mica rock. "I think I am able to make letters to form a message," Andshe told Miffit after trying a few more times. "Why not try to send the letter V to begin with and see how that works," Miffit suggested.

Everything seemed to work out just right, and Andshe was able to reflect a perfect letter V on the rock in the distance.

"What does this letter V mean anyway?" asked Andshe.

"The V letter has the 'Va' sound," Miffit said. You make this sound by placing your lower lip next to your bottom teeth and then you can hear the sound the V makes. Here, Andshe, just try it and feel the V sound as you place your lip next to your teeth."

"Only two more letters can be used in our message. The three letters we use have to make sense to Boss Mouse. He is a smart leader and will understand our code from using only three letters. We have to make sure the 'Va' sound forms a word so Boss Mouse knows we are coming home," Miffit told Andshe. "Can you think of two more letters we can use in our message to send Boss Mouse?" Miffit asked.

"Let us send the letter N as our next letter," Andshe said. "It will be easy to make using my white claw to reflect the sun to the rock."

Andshe began moving her claw back and forth in the right positions making an N on the mica rock.

"Will Boss Mouse be able to understand this one?" she asked Miffit.

"Make sure that when you reflect the sun to the mica rock, the N is made correctly," Miffit told her.

"An N is made using straight lines; however, the lines must go from left to right and not the other way or the N will appear backwards. If you make the lines going from right to left, the N will be inside out and backwards," Miffit told Andshe. "Let me help you with this one," he said.

Very carefully and deliberately together, they formed an N on the mica rock in the distance, by reflecting the sun from her white nail. "Beautiful and wonderful," they thought. "But wait, what does the N mean or stand for?" they wondered. Miffit helped Andshe make the sound of the N.

"It sounds like this" as he made the N sound. "Just place your tongue next to your top teeth when you sound out the 'N'," Miffit said. "The N, when sounded becomes 'In'. Boss Mouse will know how this sounds and what it means," Miffit said.

"We must hurry and get our third letter sent to Boss Mouse, for the sun will be going down soon," Miffit told Andshe.

"Do you think we can get our third letter sent before sundown?"

"What is our next letter going to be?" Miffit wondered.

"We must use another straight line letter and no curves," Miffit said. "Hey, how about using the letter L?"

"Great idea, but make sure that we do it correctly or we will have another mixed up letter like the backwards or inside out N," Miffit said.

"What do you mean?" Andshe wondered as she began holding her claw nail in a position to reflect the sun to the mica rock. "I should not get too mixed up on this one," she said.

"The letter L, if not correctly formed can be confusing," Miffit said. "If you make your straight line going sideways on the top and not the bottom, the L becomes a 7."

"Oh, I never thought of that!" said Andshe.

"We do not want to confuse Boss Mouse by sending combinations of letters and numbers. Our message should either contain all numbers or all letters," Miffit said.

After just one try, Andshe had formed a reflective shaped L on the mica rock. It was in perfect form, not upside down or backwards. Miffit was very impressed and pleased with how well Andshe was able to precisely hold her pinky to form the three letters of the message they had sent to Boss Mouse.

"What is our message saying?" Andshe asked Miffit.

"Well, sound out the letters and learn the code," he said. "What does the letter L sound like? You can hear and make the L sound by placing your tongue on the roof of your mouth, lips open and say L." "The L sounds like 'LUH' when said correctly," Miffit said.

"Boss Mouse will understand our message even using our three-letter code," Miffit thought. "Now when these are in order the sounds will all make sense," He thought.

Within an instant Boss Mouse had seen the message and began to place the letters in logical order to form a message. Boss Mouse always amazed everyone with how clever and wise he seemed to be. He immediately recognized the letters and their sounds and knew it was a message from Miffit. This was the first contact Miffit had been able to make with Boss Mouse and the colony in a long time. Many things had happened since Miffit was taken up in the whirlwind and relocated. Boss Mouse knew he must begin to prepare the colony for the return of Miffit. Boss Mouse gave the signal to alert his groomers they should get the secret formula and begin applying it to his whiskers. It was time for a very important meeting. When Boss Mouse requested the secret formula, the colony knew it was a very special time. It had been a while now since Boss Mouse had used the formula and called a meeting. "What is going on?" the colony wondered!

XXII
BOSS MOUSE DECODES A MESSAGE

All the colony of mice assembled, each according to their position of importance within the group. The two groomers combed and brushed every hair into the exact position for this important meeting. Boss Mouse was always in perfect form when conducting meetings. He was so particular with the position of his whiskers, this time he doubled the amount of secret formula. This was most unusual, as never before had he requested twice the amount be used to curve the top two upward, bottom two downward and the middle two straight out. His whiskers were groomed so well and covered with the formula, that they cast reflections when the sun struck them. Never before had

this amount of preparation taken place before any meeting. So much formula had been used for this special meeting, that the groomer mice wondered if they had sufficient amounts of formula for future meetings. WOW! WAS THIS SPECIAL OR WHAT?

Boss Mouse cleared his throat. This was the signal that no one moved made a sound or wiggled. All the colony had been through this many times before and understood the consequences should they not follow the rules during meeting times. They all remembered that Miffit was usually the only violator of the rules during meeting times. Some still remembered how Miffit had conducted himself during meeting times. Their memories were not favorable ones, and they tried not to think about how Miffit could be so mischievous most of the time. Boss Mouse began deliberately and specifically addressing the entire group of the colony.

"I believe I have good news," Boss Mouse began.

"It is an important day for the entire family of mice here in our new land. Most of you can remember how during our windy season some time ago you were all advised to seek shelter from those vicious winds. We all had sufficient warning when the dark black clouds blocked the sun from our view. The wind blew so terrifically hard, that dust swirled in and around, making us all close our eyes to keep the sand from getting in our eyes. I was extremely proud of the fact that all of you escaped from the danger that was present that late afternoon; well, all of you except Miffit."

Each member of the colony sat motionless, and listened as they had never listened before. Boss Mouse spoke in a much softer voice, almost like a whisper. They all were as 'quiet as a mouse' so to speak.

"Earlier today," Boss Mouse continued, "A reflection from our point of reference mica rock caught my eye. All of you know how we rely on the mica rock for our boundary limits during our hunting and gathering of food supplies. This rock has been a focal point for early warnings of wind and rainstorms for many generations. It has not only been a landmark for us but a guide for migrating birds as they use it in changing directions of travel from place to place. Something most interesting caught my eye as I was watching over the area. A series of three letters were formed on this mica rock this afternoon. I believe I know what they mean and whom they are from, but would appreciate your thoughts in assisting me in solving this code. I am going to draw these letters for you and hope that you reach the same conclusion I have made."

Never had the colony been as quiet and interested in what Boss Mouse was saying as they were now. Every mouse was so very anxious to see what Boss Mouse was going to draw for them. Each was wishing and hoping they would reach the same conclusion that Boss Mouse had been discussing with them. This was going to be a test of courage, understanding and knowledge. Perhaps Boss Mouse was going to choose a new leader for the colony in the new land, and it was a test of their ability to reason, and provide the guidance and leadership he had been looking for. Everyone's eyes were focused on the right hand of Boss Mouse as he made a symbol in the air in front of them. From the movements of his paws, they all recognized what letter he was drawing. It was a huge letter N.

They knew their letters and how they sounded from the training sessions during the past seasons. Each colony had been trained with predetermined symbols and sounds that would alert them in time of danger. Boss Mouse was an expert code designer. He understood abbreviations and contractions. He had trained the colony very well through many rehearsals in life-saving skills, using only one letter to represent larger words or small groups of words to form sentences. The past training had paid off more than once to escape danger by making only one letter in the sand, warning them all of present danger. The system had worked in the past, and they all knew now that a signal was being sent, but what was it and from whom?

After Boss Mouse made the huge N with his paws, he immediately formed the letter L in only one downward and side ways motion. Nearly everyone understood the 'N', and what it meant. Fewer mice were able to sound out and hear the L sound by placing their tongues on the roof of their mouth behind their teeth. It was getting more difficult with each letter,

but a few now understood the first two letters and what they were saying. Boss Mouse at this time was not asking for partial solutions to the message, he informed everyone that he hoped they would know the answer following his showing them the third letter he had seen early that day on the mica rock.

Not one mouse doubted for a second that Boss Mouse had imagined any part of what they had been shown with the two letters. Nearly everyone one time or the other had witnessed a reflection from the mica rock, but no one had seen anything like a message or a letter that made any sense. After all, every sunny day as the sun passed from rising in the East to setting in the West it would cast a reflection on the mica rock they had all seen and been accustomed to. Somehow, this time it was so much different. Boss Mouse would not ever play any tricks and pull pranks on the colony. He was respected for being serious, wise and a discerning leader. They all loved him. Not one single mouse did not respect, honor and obey their kind and loving leader.

Boss Mouse stood up from his position in front of the group as he formed the third and final letter. With one precise and quick downward and upward motion, a perfect V was formed for all of them to see. Only the brightest few understood what the three letters were saying. Boss Mouse could sense that some of the group understood the message. Quietly, slowly, deliberately but politely Boss Mouse asked the very few who understood the message to come to the front of the room. Three mice took a position in front of the group, one step lower than where Boss Mouse was standing.

"Do you believe you know what the letters are saying?" he asked the three mice he had called forward.

In a soft like whisper, the three simultaneously responded with, "Yes."

Boss Mouse asked them to step up to where he was and quietly whisper in his ear, their interpretations of the message. They did just that, and instantly Boss Mouse had the most pleasing look on his face.

He said, "You may now tell the rest of the group what the message was saying." The tree mice stepped down one level and one at a time and sounded out the N, L, V sounds as they had been trained in the past.

The first mouse said clearly and loudly, the N stands for "IN".

The second mouse was a bit nervous, as he had never spoken in front of any group before. He became slightly flush, not quite embarrassed as he said, "the L means LUH"   But when the third mouse began to speak, he explained, "that when you combine the L with the V, it makes the sound 'LOVE'.

Thus, the three mice cheered loudly as they said to the group, "'In love' is the message! It is coming from Miffit! He is finding his way home, and will bring a special someone home with him!"

At that announcement, cheers of joy and excitement could be heard throughout the entire colony. Dancing, singing and shouting were taking place everywhere. Boss Mouse could not have been more pleased than he was at this moment.

Boss Mouse gained control over the joyful colony of mice with a louder than usual clearing of his throat. All the mice knew when Boss Mouse cleared his throat it was time to listen. Each mouse then began to hear what Boss Mouse was going to say about the message he had seen on the mica rock that afternoon. It was difficult for the colony of mice to sit still and be quiet that afternoon. They had all missed Miffit so very much, as he had been gone a long time. This was the first sign or message they had received from Miffit since he was taken up and away in the can containing the sunflower pits. Excitement was filling the room, as Boss Mouse began to inform the group of his plan for the return of Miffit. They all hoped it would be a shorter than usual meeting, as they were anxious to help prepare for the homecoming of Miffit.

XXIII
A CELEBRATION IS PLANNED

In what seemed like minutes and minutes, but was only a few seconds until Boss Mouse began telling the colony about his plan. He told them this was going to be a very special time for the colony to have one of their favorite loved ones returning home again. Most of you can remember Miffit for his unruly and mischievous behavior, but how many can remember the good things he has done? We should focus on the positive things our family does, and not dwell on negative actions. Sure, Miffit was one that often did not follow examples of what he had been told, but that is part of growing up and being a young teenager. Miffit often turned unfavorable decisions to learning experiences that he used later in his life. All of you remember that Miffit was thinking of somewhere else to be during our instruction and learning times? Miffit has proven to us all now, that he did pay attention to our teaching. Only through learning and knowing letters and words was Miffit able to send me three coded letters with so much meaning. Not only did Miffit learn his lessons early in life, but used them for his own experiences as a teenager.

"I am so proud of Miffit," Boss Mouse said.

"It is time for a celebration like no other!" said Boss Mouse.

"Miffit will join us in a few days. It is important we all take watch on the mica rock for any additional message from Miffit. It is not possible to send a message back to Miffit as he and his companion will be traveling most of time. You must remain in one location to receive any message from the mica rock. It was fortunate that I had not taken my snooze that afternoon the message came from Miffit. Had I been sleeping we all would have missed this most important message. I am so very pleased that Miffit was able to send information to us," Boss Mouse said.

"Everyone will be needed to help with the planning of this special event. No time must be wasted, please help in any way you can."

Even though Boss Mouse never did specifically state what the special occasion was, every single mouse in the colony knew in his or her mind what was going to happen. After all, why would any one send message saying or meaning they were in love and not expect to have a wedding? Yes, that was it; Boss Mouse would have to plan for a wedding. There were so many things to be done in such a short period of time! Boss Mouse did mention there would be a celebration, yes of course a wedding celebration. But wait; what's the name of the bride and where was she from? Boy did rumors fly throughout the colony that afternoon! Boss Mouse was going to require some assistance in getting everything accomplished before the wedding day. He called for his special workers and thinkers to help with all the planning. Boss Mouse secretly hoped that Miffit could provide more details to assist with planning for a wedding. "Maybe I should spend another afternoon in the sun and see if another message might be sent for me to decipher," he thought.

Evening times were spent preparing food and making nests for the nighttime rest that followed their busy days. This evening was different. It seemed like no one wanted to rest or relax after the Western sunset. Anticipation and excitement were running through the minds of every mouse that evening. Each one was thinking about how he or she could help with the planning. Even the youngest mice were figuring out what they could do to make this wedding special. Several very young mice began asking Mrs. Mouse what they could do to help. Mrs. Mouse in her loving way always could find meaningful helping tasks that even the smallest mouse could do. The young mice felt so very special after Mrs. Mouse gave them responsibilities to make them feel grown up and important.

"It is time for resting now," Boss Mouse told the group. "Tomorrow is special and important to us, let us not tire out tonight and not be able to work in the morning." "I will provide the plan after we have our morning meal," he said. Boss Mouse was more excited than everyone combined, but as their leader could not let his feelings influence important, wise, and well thought out decisions. Boss Mouse was asleep in just a few minutes. Not even the thunderstorms that passed through that evening were loud enough to waken the overly tired leader.

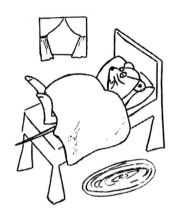

"We must have music," said Boss Mouse the next morning after breakfast. "I know that some of you can make unique sounds with your voice. We all joined together and made a sound like a barking dog when we lived under the haystack near the farmer's field. It was necessary to scare off that old ugly cat that always bothered us. Most of you can remember that Miffit had his tail broken by a paw from that nasty old cat. We all joined in to make sounds like never before, to protect ourselves.

"Why not practice to make a wedding sound with our voices?" suggested Boss Mouse.

In an instant, several teenaged mice offered to help prepare a song for the wedding and return of Miffit. Boss Mouse was somewhat uncertain about what kind of lyrics teenager mice might arrange, but agreed to have them help with the music.

Mrs. Mouse thought it would be nice to have flowers to welcome home Miffit and his companion. She knew how to find the most fragrant ones, and a safe way to get there. "I can be responsible for flowers," she told Boss Mouse.

"Will that include the flower mouse too?" he asked her.

Mrs. Mouse said she had already been thinking of a special little mouse to be the flower mouse. Boss Mouse was okay with that notion and left all the planning up to Mrs. Mouse. She was delighted and pleased to think she could be of so much help. She would have to ask for some help from her sisters and cousins to make sure everything was done correctly and on time.

Boss Mouse hoped Miffit would return soon from his journey. Boss Mouse was getting older now and growing more tired earlier in the evening than he had in the past. He was not sure how much longer he could effectively provide the wisdom and guidance to the growing colony. This had been a worry for him, as decisions affecting so many ages and areas of interest were becoming more difficult to provide to the expanding colony. Boss Mouse had done his best in keeping current with needs of younger mice and their special needs, which seemed to him unending. Perhaps it was time to select another leader. But who would this be? And, when?

"We just saw a reflection of something white and beautiful on the mica rock," a group of teenaged mice ran in and reported to Boss Mouse.

"Send out a scout immediately," Boss Mouse requested to his closest attendants. "Let me know what you hear or see." He hoped it was going to be another message or signal from Miffit, perhaps about when he would come home, and with whom. Boy, wouldn't that be special to learn his girlfriend's name?

The scouts returned to let Boss Mouse know what they had learned from the mica reflections. "The colors were bright," they said. "We saw reds, pinks and pure white," they told Boss Mouse. Boss Mouse could not think of anything both white and beautiful. What could it be? The eyes on Boss Mouse squinted for just a split second. He stroked his upper whiskers gently, while his lower whiskers pointed downward. He rubbed them until they shone in the bright sun light, all the time thinking about what pink, red and pure white might stand for. Calmly but respectfully, Boss Mouse said, "It is a white furry mouse wearing a red and pink set of clothing." Boss Mouse continued to amaze members of the mouse colony with his wisdom. "How could Boss Mouse always have the answer to everything?" they wondered.

Many older members of the colony were anticipating what was going to happen next. They had been hearing about pure white and furry, colorful styles of clothing and something pretty was accompanying Miffit on his homebound journey. Several teenaged mice were speculating that a wedding was going to happen when Miffit and his friend arrived back in the new land. They wondered what this new friend was going to be like, and began to worry about whether they would like each other. Boss Mouse had taught all the colony of mice good manners and how to be polite to others. He often told them if you were kind to a new friend, you would be some day blessed for the kindness you have shown. Some of the younger mice had experienced goodness and love paid to them for their service and consideration to others. Boss Mouse was a great leader that they all loved.

XXIV
RED-BELLIED FLYERS MESSAGE

The next morning was a busy one. It was very overcast with heavy rain clouds in the sky above. They all knew that this meant no reflections from the mica rock were possible today. Eagerly they began with their routines and daily activities, in hope that the wind would blow the clouds away so the sun could shine. All were anxious to see another message on the mica rock. Just in case the sun would come from behind the clouds and make a reflection, Boss Mouse posted his most senior scout at the lookout position. That senior scout had an important mission, but was well trained and prepared for what might take place. He had received instruction and learned from examples given to him by Boss Mouse on methods of proper scouting. The senior scout took his job very seriously, as he watched constantly for any glare on the mica rock.

Some time during the middle of the afternoon, Boss Mouse observed several red breasted and light red-bellied birds circling and circling just above the area where he was taking a short rest. The more he watched these low flying birds he noticed specific flight patterns. The birds were flying in such a way, that with little imagination, you could see they were forming letters and words in the blue sky. Boss Mouse was amazed to learn that the patterns of flight from these little red-bellied flyers were giving him a message. What could this message be and from whom was it coming? Boss Mouse understood the thoughts of other animals and many birds. He had never experienced anything like this before. Would he require some

assistance? Boss Mouse knew from experience that it is wise to think about the mysteries before trying to explain them. He closed his eyes for a few moments trying to reflect on past experience to determine how to decipher this message from the red-bellied flyers.

After watching the red-bellied flyers, the senior scout had some idea about what the messages were saying. Boss Mouse was interested in hearing what the senior scout wanted to tell him. In haste, the scout began plotting theories about what the red-breasted birds were trying to convey to the colony of mice. Boss Mouse was giving the scout some of his attention while listening to him, but had his own theory of what was taking place. The senior scout seemed to ramble and make little sense when trying to explain to Boss Mouse what he had seen. Boss Mouse listened quietly and patiently while the scout gave him his own thoughts.

Boss Mouse would never embarrass or humiliate anyone. He was a loving and kind leader that always took time to listen to members of his colony. He realized that the scout had witnessed an important event and did not want to weaken his enthusiasm. From looks on his face, clearing of his throat, or shining his whiskers Boss Mouse knew he was in a position of authority and could easily intimidate the scout. Never would Boss Mouse intentionally hurt anyone. He was loved by many and respected by them all. This would be a good time to offer positive support to the young senior scout.

"So what did you see and what does it mean?" Boss Mouse asked the scout.

The scout told Boss Mouse that flying birds were making formations in forms of arrows and hearts. "It was really neat, as they were all flying in a group shaped like an arrow going through a heart. It was difficult at times to see because the clouds were blocking some of the view. Nevertheless, these little red-bellied flyers repeated and repeated the same patterns over and over again. I think they are trying to tell us something, but not quite sure what it might be."

"Do you have any ideas?" the scout asked Boss Mouse.

"Try to watch more closely and see if other birds are acting strangely also," said Boss Mouse.

"During times like this most species of the same kind respond in similar ways. Since these birds were flying low in the air, we might want to watch for the high fliers to see if they are trying to send us a signal as well."

The scout said he would return early the next morning and watch for the high flyers. Boss Mouse had taught all the mice to beware of the flat flyers in the past, so the scout would seek a safe hiding place where he could watch the birds but not be seen by them.

"Try to find out what direction those birds are heading also, as this could be an important clue to understanding their message," Boss Mouse suggested to the scout.

Just as the sun was rising in the East the next morning, flocks of low and high fliers were circling and circling above the new land. Not only were the scouts looking toward the sky, but most of the other mice in the colony were also recognizing lines that formed into letters. The letters became words for the colony of mice to read from the ground, as they looked skyward. The signals from the flight patterns were all the same now. More arrows with hearts through them, flapping wings made soothing sounds while their songs were pleasing and easy to understand and listen to. The melody was catchy, words easily understood with rhythmic formations being formed by flying birds above. Everyone knew and fully understood what this all was meaning. It was a happy time for the entire colony. Soon most

of the mice were either humming or singing familiar song words given to them from the circling birds.

Boss Mouse knew that he would need assistance in organizing an event like the homecoming for Miffit. He thought and thought about how to find the name of Miffit's' friend. He knew the birds were teaching songs to the mouse family and if he honed in on their lyrics he just might get a clue about the name of Miffit's new friend. He might learn something about her too. This all would help with planning the wedding that was going to take place as soon as Miffit returned. Boss Mouse dined on special ripe berries and nuts that evening before taking a well-deserved rest.

"Tomorrow is a new day, full of ideas and blessing for everyone," he thought. "I will trust that I will be shown and told what to get done for Miffit and his gal pal."

Nights are so long when you have a lot on your mind as Boss Mouse had that night. Boss Mouse always rested better after a full tummy and fresh water to drink. He hoped that a dream might come true for him and reveal the secrets that Miffit was trying to send to him. Boss Mouse shut his eyes only for a few seconds he thought, but awoke some hours later from the bright sun coming up under the light clouds above.

And they flew higher, *and* they flew faster Boss Mouse thought early the next morning. *And* they are beautiful, *and* their bellies are bright red, *and* they sing so softly.   "WAIT, I have the answer!" Boss Mouse said to himself.

"Her name is Andshe. And she is beautiful, and she can sing, and she can do so many things. Miffit and Andshe will make a new life together. All those hearts and arrows are signals that those two are in love and planning a life together."

Boss Mouse was more pleased than ever before as his dreams had been answered. He understood what the birds had been telling them, and now more than ever the mica rock messages took special meanings.

"Wonderful! Great! I am so happy!" he thought. Maybe some of the lessons Boss Mouse tried to teach Miffit when he was younger had paid off. "Miffit was a mischievous little fellow," Boss Mouse thought to himself, "but somehow I was sure he would turn out just right."

XXV
MIFFIT AND ANDSHE COME HOME

Boss Mouse now understood the message and songs from the birds, and all the mica rock reflections that Miffit had been sending to the colony. "We must make plans for a wedding and a special homecoming, as Miffit and Andshe will soon be married. It will be a very important times for us all," Boss Mouse thought.

"We must collect the finest berries and nuts for this feast that will be taking place in a couple of days," Boss Mouse told everyone.

"Miffit and Andshe are nearly home now; let each of us begin to prepare to make this wedding the best one ever," Boss Mouse thought.

Boss Mouse cleared his throat this time much louder than ever before. All the mice in the colony understood the importance of being in their respective positions when Boss Mouse cleared his throat. Every one scurried to get to their assigned position of importance within the group before they were given that special look of rejection from Boss Mouse. Boss Mouse was the most important mouse in the colony, and all the others knew he did not appreciate waiting for them to get into their position for his meetings. "It was like magic," Mrs. Mouse thought to herself, "how quickly the entire colony assembled for the meeting." Boss Mouse was so excited to address the colony that he did not ask the groomer to fix his six whiskers in their positions. He did not even use the secret formula or brush his fur like meetings in the past. Everyone wondered, "What could have a higher priority than brushed fur or secret formula used on whiskers?"

Boss Mouse told the group that he learned the name of Miffit's companion while watching and listening to the red-bellied fliers above. He knew they were trying to send signals by the formations formed, and the songs they had been singing.

"I am so pleased to let you know that Miffit is going to marry Andshe." She was given the name Andshe because she does so many things." *And she* can sing, *and she* can dance *and she* can play, *and she* can gather the finest seeds, *and she* also wears eyeliner, *and she* paints her paw nails. The low flying birds gave me all these clues about her, it just took me a few days of very hard thinking and deciphering to understand what they were saying. She must be a beautiful pure white mouse that Miffit has chosen for his wife. In only two more days of traveling, they will be here with us. We have many things to get done. Each of you knows how you can help; using your talent and skills that you learned living in the colony."

"If any need special assistance or further instruction, let me know," said Boss Mouse. "The meeting is finished. Let us all get to work in making their wedding a huge success."

Miffit and Andshe were making very good time traveling back to the new land. Light showers of rain were reducing the need to find water, and a slow and gentle breeze kept them from getting too hot and tired out. They were able to find fresh nuts and berries to eat which also prevented them from getting overly hungry. Andshe, however, did not eat some of the ripest berries, which seemed strange to Miffit. He, of course, gobbled them down so quickly it was as if he never had eaten in days. Miffit always thought of his stomach first, appearance later. Andshe was just the opposite. She squeezed the juice from the ripe berries and used it to paint her nails.

Her philosophy was to look pretty and eat later. Andshe told Miffit that that is the way fashionable mice live. He still thought his way was the best of all, and continued to eat all he could.

"What is that to the West in front of us?" Andshe asked Miffit.

"Hey! That is a landmark next to where the colony lives," Miffit told her. "We are very near the two towers where the scouts keep watch for visitors. It will only be a short while now till we arrive in the new land," Miffit said.

"The scouts should have seen and reported to Boss Mouse by now that we are nearly home. If we rush just a bit more, we can arrive before the evening meal. I know you will like eating with my family. They are so clever in how they gather seeds, nuts and berries. You will be so pleased to learn our method of preparing meals and eating with one another. It is like a ritual, each one has their position of importance in seating arrangements. The closer you eat next to Boss Mouse the more important you become in the family group. Since I was in trouble most of the time I ate my food a long way from Boss Mouse," Miffit told Andshe. "I still loved him nonetheless, and know that what he did to me was for the best. It just took me some growing up to realize how wise and full of wisdom Boss Mouse really is."

Miffit recognized voices from the shouts of jubilant rejoicing that was chanted from the colony. Over and over again, members of the colony were singing happy songs to show their appreciation for the homecoming of Miffit and his companion Andshe. Miffit was able to make out the words of their songs as he listened to what they were saying. These words and tunes were familiar as Miffit even learned some from the red-bellied fliers that once circled over and over him. He began to hum the tune as the words ran through his mind. After just a couple times through Andshe joined him in singing along with members of the colony. It goes like this; Miffit thought:

Miffit and Andshe began singing along even a tune using their name as they listened to members of the colony sing other verses.

Boss Mouse

Roxie Chowen

Boss Mouse! Leader of the Colony,
Boss Mouse! Whiskers long and shiny,
Boss Mouse! Only one the mice can listen to.

Miffit! Always the adventurer,
Miffit! Hearing what he wants to hear,
Miffit! Getting into trouble once again!

Mean Cat! Look out, here he comes again,
Mean Cat! Wants to be nobody's friend,
Mean Cat! Everybody's scared when he is near!

Mrs. Mouse! Watches over everyone,
Mrs. Mouse! Keeps a neat and tidy home,
Mrs. Mouse! Doctoring whoever needs the care.

Wise Owl! There he is up in a tree,
Wise Owl! Now he's looking down at me,
Wise Owl! Helping me to know where I should go.

Old Mouse! Snapper bit off half his ear,
Old Mouse! Now it's hard for him to hear,
Old Mouse! Heed the warning his words have for you.

Hoodlums! Walk around and think they're cool,
Hoodlums! Mean and make up their own rules,
Hoodlums! Too bad they don't really know what's fun

Gophie! Host to all the family,
Gophie! Tells the mice just how to flee,
Gophie! To the mice he was a friend indeed!

Turtle! The right one has a droopy eye,
Turtle! The wrong one really makes you cry,
Turtle! His tummy has on it a secret map!

Stylish Mice! Look the same except for clothes,
Stylish Mice! White as white down to their toes,
Stylish Mice! Plan the outfits they would like to wear.

AndShe! Really can do anything,
AndShe! Sweet as flowers in the spring,
AndShe! No wonder Miffit fell in love with her!

XXVI
BOSS MOUSE AND ANDSHE MEET

"Miffit, how should I honor and respect Boss Mouse when I first meet him?" Andshe asked. "You have told me so much about how full of wisdom and knowledge Boss Mouse is, I could be uneasy during our first meeting. I want to give him the respect he has earned and deserved from all the colony of mice. If you would give me some things to say or ideas on how to act appropriately, I would appreciate it," Andshe said.

Andshe was overwhelmed as she watched the entire colony of mice parade towards her and Miffit that afternoon as they cheered and sang songs of joy. Andshe did not have any time to think about what to say or how to greet Boss Mouse, as it all happened so quickly. There she was, face to face, greeting Boss Mouse himself. He made her feel so welcome to the group. It was just as Miffit had told her. Boss Mouse was everything Miffit had described and even more. Andshe was very impressed with the smooth fur, manicured whiskers and the wisdom that seemed to exude from Boss Mouse.

"I am honored and pleased to meet you today," Andshe said as she touched the paw of Boss Mouse.

"The pleasure is all mine, Andshe," Boss Mouse responded as he took a shallow bow of respect. "Will you please be my special guest this afternoon?"

Andshe, Miffit and Boss Mouse were in the front of the colony as they proceeded to the meeting place in the new land. It was not necessary to have Boss Mouse clear his throat to begin this meeting. All colony members were seated immediately, eagerly and anxiously waiting for the introduction of Andshe to the group. She was so beautiful, eyes slightly lined to accent the blue surrounding the jet-black dot in the middle of her eyes. Her nails were colored with pale pink and rosy red juice from the ripest berries she and Miffit had found early that morning. Her fur was the color of new fallen snow, with every hair meticulously in its place. The sun's reflection from her ivory colored pinky nail sent sparkling beams of light across the room. Her tail was so perfectly shaped, she was the envy of every young female mouse in the group. Her voice was harmonic and melodious. When she spoke, ever so softly, everyone gave full attention to her.

"Members of the group, this is Andshe," Boss Mouse said.

"Please help me in welcoming her to our colony."

Before Boss Mouse had finished the sentence, cheers of excitement roared throughout the entire colony. Some younger members began to dance around and sing, others jumped up and down while a few just sat back and smiled. This was the most exciting event anyone could remember. It was going to be the most special time for the entire colony.

Boss Mouse again addressed the group, "Let us have the wedding tonight for Miffit and Andshe."

Miffit for once used his best behavior to impress not only Andshe but also all the friends and family of the mouse colony during the wedding. He had asked Boss Mouse for just a little dab of the secret formula to be used on his fur, and only a dash on his five and ½ whiskers. Boss Mouse agreed to let Miffit use the formula only because he was getting married. Miffit was informed that under no other circumstance could the formula ever be used by anyone except

Boss Mouse himself. Miffit felt so very proud knowing that he was the only other mouse to use the formula. And, did it ever make him special!

Miffit stood tall and straight wrapping his crooked tail around his feet to hide the obvious hook that no other mouse had in its tail. He twisted and wrapped his top and bottom whisker in such a way with the formula that the ½ whisker blended with the other whiskers. His fur was brushed and combed to perfection; he could not have looked any finer for the wedding. He grinned and smiled, his chest was puffed out with enthusiasm. "I am ready to be a married mouse," he thought to himself. "I think so much of Andshe, I cannot imagine another day without her being my wife."

Andshe looked marvelous. She smelled of fragrance from a recipe taught to her by using juice from squeezing ripened berries. No other mouse had smelled that way or so good. It was pleasing and relaxing to take a breath and breathe in that soothing smell that Andshe was wearing for the wedding. Her fur was silky smooth. Her complexion was radiant and the look in her eyes was heavenly. She wanted to be called Mrs. Miffit she felt, but she knew how much

Miffit liked to call her Andshe. She knew when Boss Mouse introduced her as Andshe that that should be her given name.

"The ceremony will now begin," Boss Mouse said with authority.

Andshe faced Miffit. As she looked at Miffit with those soft warm and inviting eyes, a tiny tear formed in his eye that everyone noticed. It was a tear of support showing his admiration of Andshe and what she meant to him. Miffit could hardly be heard that afternoon as he said the "I do's and I will's" as Boss Mouse asked him to do.

"Do you, Andshe, take Miffit" ………..,,,

Therefore, the wedding ceremony was completed that afternoon.

Boss Mouse said, "I now want to introduce to you - Mr. and Mrs. Miffit."

Miffit and Andshe were the most beautiful couple anyone had ever seen. They fit so well together, everyone wished them the very best as they scurried out of the meeting place to begin their honeymoon. Andshe told Miffit that they should take a honeymoon for the rest of their lives. Miffit thought that would be a great idea. The entire colony waved and sang until they no longer could be seen or heard as Miffit and Andshe walked away hand in hand toward the setting sun in the West.

ABOUT THE AUTHOR

Dennis Chowen, a naturalized American citizen, born in Canada, and raised and educated in the Midwest, is a former elementary school teacher and principal, holding a Masters Degree in Education. He spent a decade in the education field before entering a career with the US Army.

During his first career, he served as five/sixth grade teacher, storyteller, and principal. He holds a lifetime membership in the National Education Assoc., initiated a GED program, was president of the local teacher's association, nominated for Outstanding Principal, and is now on the School Board for the third largest area-wide district in the US.

He has recently retired from his second career with the United States Army at the rank of Lieutentant Colonel. During this time, he served on three continents and traveled to more than 40 countries. In his off-duty hours, he could be found entertaining and delighting children thru his storytelling in youth centers, clubs, and chapel organizations. Upon retirement, he was awarded the Legion of Merit, the 5th highest peacetime award.

He was inspired for the writing of Boss Mouse by a former student, Mrs. Cari Frazier, who invited him to tell a weekly story to her second grade class.

He resides in Sturgis, SD, with his wife, Roxie, who is a musician and composer of the Boss Mouse theme song. Their neighbor and close friend, Jeanine Harms, is the illustrator and co-lyricist for the song. Dennis and Roxie have three adult children living in VA and FL.

Printed in the United States
45464LVS00006B/394-444

9 781420 890761